Janice Lynn has a Masters in Nursing from Vanderbilt University, and works as a nurse practitioner in a family practice. She lives in the southern United States with her husband, their four children, their Jack Russell—appropriately named Trouble—and a lot of unnamed dust bunnies that have moved in since she started her writing career. To find out more about Janice and her writing visit janicelynn.com.

Also by Janice Lynn

The ER's Newest Dad
After the Christmas Party...
Flirting with the Doc of Her Dreams
New York Doc to Blushing Bride
Winter Wedding in Vegas
Sizzling Nights with Dr Off-Limits
It Started at Christmas...
The Nurse's Baby Secret
The Doctor's Secret Son
A Firefighter in Her Stocking

Discover more at millsandboon.co.uk.

A SURGEON TO HEAL HER HEART

BY
JANICE LYNN

MILLS & BOON

Published in Great Britain 2018
by Mills & Boon, an imprint of HarperCollins*Publishers*
1 London Bridge Street, London, SE1 9GF

© 2018 Janice Lynn

ISBN: 978-0-263-93337-6

Printed and bound in Spain
by CPI, Barcelona

To all those caring for loved ones with chronic illnesses.

CHAPTER ONE

"I'M TELLING YOU, that man has the hots for you."

At her co-worker's words, the corners of nurse Carly Evans' lips inched upward. Still, she shrugged as if the comment was no big deal. She needed to fight the excitement Rosalyn's claim incited, not give her heart free rein to jump up and down with joy.

Jump up and down? Ha. More like her heart was somersaulting worthy of a world-class medal.

The same flip-flopping routine her heart went into any time she thought of the hospital's newest general surgeon.

Not that she had a right to feel that way. Not when she couldn't do one thing about her heart's acrobatics or any hots Dr. Stone Parker might have for her.

Stone.

Just thinking his name, how his eyes, his mouth had immediately crinkled with a smile when they'd met hers on this morning's rounds, had her blood pounding. The erratic rhythm practically demanded a giddy schoolgirl dance with fists thrust into the air.

Maybe her friend should be saying Carly had the hots for Stone.

She did.

For all the good it would do her.

Which was the problem.

She'd have been better off if she'd never met Stone,

never felt the way he made every nerve cell inside her hum with life.

That she wasn't free hadn't been a problem, until she'd met him. Now...now, she was torn and hated herself for it.

Closing the medicine cart and nearly dropping the medications she'd just taken out, Carly took a long, steadying breath, and grimaced.

"Uh-huh, I saw that so don't go pretending you're immune to the man." Rosalyn's dark brown eyes glowed with eagerness at Carly's tell-tale motion. "I've seen you two talking, the sparks that fly back and forth. You like him, too. Admit it."

Wasn't that the same as saying she liked to breathe? How could any sane, straight woman not like Stone? The man was gorgeous and the total package.

Just over six feet tall, dark brown hair with the slightest hint of curl, green eyes that twinkled when he smiled, and a face that had inspired numerous fantasies... Yeah, Stone was 'likable'.

Just a tad.

"He seems to be a great doctor and, of course, he's a good-looking man." Understatements of the year. "I can appreciate that, just as most females, including yourself, can," Carly pointed out, using all her willpower to keep her voice level, cool, and as unaffected as possible. "But that does not mean I 'like him' like him."

Like liking Stone was a waste of emotions she didn't have to spare.

"Honey, you're protesting too much." Chuckling, Rosalyn practically rubbed her hands with glee. "Admit it. He makes you all hot beneath your nursing uniform."

Carly rolled her eyes at the nurse she'd worked side by side with for the past five years. Rosalyn was a big-hearted African American woman raising four teenagers with her mechanic husband. There was no one Carly would rather work with than the long-time med-surg nurse.

Except maybe for this moment. None of her other co-workers would initiate this particular conversation.

Squaring her shoulders, Carly stared straight into her friend's dark eyes.

"I'm sure Dr. Parker is a very nice man." He was. "I enjoy our conversations very much." She did. "But whether or not he has the hots for me is totally irrelevant." Sadly, the truth. "I'm not interested in a relationship with him, or anyone else, outside these hallowed walls." Also, sadly, the truth.

Inside the hospital walls Carly was a very different person from who she was outside them.

Inside these walls she could focus on being a shining light to her patients and cling to the shadows of the Carly she'd once been.

Part of her worried *that* Carly was shriveling into nothingness to disappear forever. Which might be why she enjoyed time around Stone so much. He gave her glimpses of a younger, carefree version of herself.

Made her insides spark as if trying to relight a fire that used to brightly burn. In her fantasies, it still did.

In the real world, that fire couldn't be relit. Unfortunately.

"Why is that?"

Carly jumped at the question that came from behind her. Literally and figuratively. *What? How?*

She'd been expecting Rosalyn to respond, not the familiar masculine voice that had the effect of morphing her insides to melted butter.

When had he walked up behind her?

Why hadn't Rosalyn told her?

Or at least given some indication he was on the medical floor and within earshot? She had to have seen him behind Carly.

Rosalyn had set her up, playing matchmaker.

Slowly, Carly turned to face the man she'd just been talking about.

Insides quaking, she stared into the most beautiful green eyes she'd ever encountered. So green she could almost be convinced the color was the result of contact lenses. If she'd had any doubts, he was now close enough to put that question to rest. All she could see was gorgeous bright green eyes, the color of spring bringing life back after a long cold spell.

Dark, long lashes fringed his eyes, giving them a surreal look that only added to his already handsome face. No doubt about it. Stone was easy to look at.

She opened her mouth, meaning to tell him something, anything, but not the truth.

The truth was something she kept private. Something she didn't talk about with her co-workers because she needed to keep her life compartmentalized. At the hospital, she worked hard, was free to laugh with her co-workers and patients, to just feel normal and pretend life was grand.

She wouldn't let home creep into work.

She couldn't.

Not if any part of her was to survive.

Compartmentalization was her friend and kept her sane.

"Yeah," Rosalyn added, her amused gaze bouncing back and forth between Stone and Carly.

Her co-worker was definitely having Cupid inclinations. In another lifetime, Carly would have welcomed her help, would have welcomed a man like Stone being interested. Welcomed and been over the moon. But that wasn't where she was and probably wouldn't be for years.

Lord, she hoped it would be years.

The alternative was unthinkable.

Stone's gaze cut to the grinning nurse who was watching them with the eagerness of a movie-goer. All she needed was a seat and some popcorn.

"Rosalyn, would you mind getting a warm blanket for

Room 207?" he asked. "That's what I stepped out to do, but fortunately I ran into you lovely ladies."

Carly was one hundred percent sure "fortunately" was not what she'd call him overhearing her and Rosalyn's conversation.

Heat flooded Carly's face and she glanced down at her tennis shoes, staring at the neon-green laces. Good work shoes were the one luxury she allowed herself. With the long hours she worked, good shoes mattered.

"Yes, sir." Rosalyn grinned at him, and then winked at Carly. Chuckling, she took off toward where the blanket warmer was located. "Just you remember what I said, Carly Evans," she called without turning around. "It would do you some good to think about that."

Carly was pretty sure her cheeks were as red as her scrubs. Maybe more so as her scrubs were a little faded from too many washings.

When Rosalyn was out of earshot, Stone turned back to Carly. One side of his mouth lifted in a wry smile. "I didn't intentionally listen in, but will admit that I'm intrigued by what I heard. You mind explaining?"

She minded. "How much did you hear?"

"Enough to know I want to hear more."

Being careful not to spill Room 204's medication from the cup, Carly put her hands on her hips. "Which tells me nothing."

"How much could I have overheard?" His eyes twinkled.

Good grief, he'd heard everything. Was the fact that he was standing behind Carly why Rosalyn had mentioned him in the first place?

"Not a lot." Carly decided to go for nonchalant. Nonchalant was good and meant she didn't care what he'd overheard. He didn't know her private thoughts, nor would he ever. "Rosalyn had a theory about you. I told her that her theory was pointless as I wasn't interested in anything beyond friendship."

"Which is where I asked why you weren't interested." His lips twitched, his eyes sparkled, and he was enjoying that he'd caught her having a conversation about him.

"Yes," she said for lack of knowing what else to say, a little flustered by the fact Stone didn't mind that Rosalyn had said he had the hots for Carly. Which meant what?

That he did have the hots for her?

He'd flirted, but he was such a good-natured person, talking with everyone, so she'd consoled herself that her talking back was harmless, that nothing would come of their shared conversations. He wouldn't really be interested in her outside of having a little fun at the hospital.

He was a gorgeous doctor. She was just her. An overworked, over-stressed, financially stretched nurse doing all she could to provide care for her seriously ill mother.

"You didn't answer my question," he pointed out, his intent gaze warning she'd been fooling herself on thinking their conversations didn't mean anything.

Her pulse drummed rapidly at her temple.

"I wasn't having a discussion with you," she reminded him, knowing she had to get her thoughts, her reaction to him, under control. Better to stay in denial than to acknowledge what she couldn't have, what she couldn't let herself have. "You weren't a part of the conversation you interrupted."

She wanted to be irritated with him, but how could anyone be upset with him when he had such an all-encompassing smile on his face? A smile that crinkled the corners of his eyes, dug dimples into his cheeks, and made his eyes sparkle?

Good grief. The man was incorrigible. And so gorgeous. And so out of her reach. Still, the way he made her feel was addictive, like a magic spell that gave everything a shiny glow.

A shiny glow she'd like to bask in, but life had other

plans for her. Plans that didn't include time for a dalliance with the most intriguing man she'd ever met.

She arched a brow and shook her head. "Some would say eavesdropping was rude, you know?"

His left dimple dug a little deeper. "I'm part of the conversation now."

She rolled her eyes upward. "Not by my choice."

He laughed. "You saying I'm holding you here against your will?"

Carly shrugged. "Obviously not. If you'll excuse me?" She went to push past him.

"I won't."

Eyes wide, Carly stopped, met his for once serious gaze. "Pardon?"

"I won't excuse you," he clarified. "Not this time. Eavesdropping was rude. You're right. But since I was the topic of conversation, surely I'm forgiven for jumping in?"

Her insides shook so that she still might end up spilling those meds she held yet. "There's no rule that says I have to forgive you for butting into my conversation."

"Even when the conversation is about me?"

"Especially when the conversation is about you."

He chuckled. "You should have dinner with me tonight and let me convince you to forgive my so-called rudeness. Plus, we can discuss why my having the hots for you doesn't matter because it matters a great deal to me."

Guilt hit Carly. This was her fault. She should have put a stop to whatever sparks Rosalyn said were flying between them but she'd not dared to believe he was really interested in her.

Sure, he'd gone out of his way to start conversations, asking her things he could have asked any hospital employee. He'd sat back in the break room with her a few times while she'd quickly swallowed down whatever she'd packed from home.

His sitting with her while she ate should have made her

horribly uncomfortable, but instead she'd found herself regretting how quickly her short lunch break had slipped by while they'd talked. He'd asked about her favorite parts of Memphis and, drawing upon her childhood and college memories, she'd told him. No need to tell him that for five years she'd not been to any of those places. Surely, they hadn't changed that much in such a short time?

Then again, she'd changed that much.

Aged a hundred years, at least.

But for all that, she'd thought their interactions innocent. She'd figured Stone had svelte, glamorous women lined up in droves out there in the real world. Talking with Carly was just a fun way to pass time when he was at work.

Had she really believed that?

Or had she refused to believe anything else because she enjoyed his attention and hadn't wanted to give it up?

She didn't lead on men when she had no intentions of following through. So if he was interested then, yeah, she had to put a halt to it right now.

Carly's throat tightened as she said, "Our discussing that would be an utter waste of both of our time."

"I've time to spare."

"That makes one of us." She seriously doubted he had much time to spare, either.

His dark brow arched. "You're too busy to go to dinner with me tonight?"

"Absolutely." She took off toward her patient's room, but he stayed in step beside her.

"Tomorrow night?"

"Busy."

Her answer seemed to waylay him for a few seconds, but then, still beside her, he asked, "Surely you make time to eat, Carly? I'll take you to the restaurant of your choice and promise to have you home at a decent hour." He waggled his brows and gave another crooked smile. "Unless you want me to keep you out past bedtime, that is."

Oh, my. Not going to happen… But, oh, my, oh, my, oh, my.

She ate in quick snatches after getting home, usually soup or a peanut butter and jelly sandwich while Joyce filled her in on the day's events.

Carly liked uneventful days.

Days in which her mother didn't have any angry outbursts or falls or screams of pain or significant declines in her failing health. It had been so long since Carly had eaten out at a restaurant that she didn't have a favorite. Money was tight. Eating out was expensive. There would be time for such luxuries later, after her mother's life succumbed to her illness.

Just as there would be time for relationships. For real relationships and smiles and going to restaurants with handsome men.

The odds of a man as fabulous as Stone ever asking her to dinner again was next to nil, but, even so, dinner dates, or staying out past bedtime, had to wait.

Carly prayed that would be many years down the road. Those snatches of good spells with her mother were worth everything. They were getting further and further in between, but on a day of clarity Carly's heart filled with enough joy to tide her over until the next brief glimpse.

Thoughts of her mother, of the fact she wasn't free to date, that to pretend otherwise with Stone was wrong, made a new wave of guilt hit her. She'd been wrong to ever let things get to this point, but it was too late to undo that now. Other than to put an abrupt stop to his interest.

As difficult as it was going to be, she had to cut all ties with Stone.

"I eat," she admitted, not that that was in question. She stopped mid-hallway to glare in as much annoyance at him as she could muster. "But not with strangers."

"I'm not a stranger," he clarified, not seeming fazed by her glare.

No wonder. It wasn't easy to glare at a gorgeous man smiling and trying to convince you to go to dinner. Maybe he could see right through her, could see that everything female inside her responded to him. Maybe he saw how much she longed for a different set of life circumstances that would mean she could have her mother and a relationship. No matter. That wasn't the life she'd been given and she wouldn't bemoan things she had no control over.

"And, we have eaten together," he reminded her, his grin full of charm. "In the break room at lunch when I'm lucky enough to catch you there. Plus, we've been working together for almost a month. We are not strangers."

He made a valid argument, but none of which made any impact on why she couldn't go to dinner.

"A whole month since you came to work at Memphis Memorial? Time does fly." To make her point, she glanced at her watch, then gave him the sternest expression she could muster. "My patient is due his medication and I am going to administer it now. Thank you for the invitation, but my answer is no and won't change." She met his gaze. "I'm sorry if I ever gave you reason to think otherwise."

He looked ready to say something more, but didn't attempt to stop her when she moved past him to hightail her way down the hospital-floor hallway.

No matter. She could feel his gaze as she hurried to escape into her patient's room and away from the most disconcerting man she'd ever met.

Tony had sure never gotten her worked up the way Stone had in the month she'd known him.

One month, four days. That was how long Stone had been at Memphis Memorial.

Not that she was counting.

She shouldn't be aware the man existed outside that he was a doctor at the hospital where she worked.

But she was aware.

Too aware.

With that thought she bit the inside of her lower lip and fought the urge to cry a little. A lot. No matter.

She had a good life, had her mother, anything beyond that would have to wait for a day she prayed never came.

Stone Parker wasn't sure how he'd misread what was happening between him and Carly Evans.

He'd thought they shared a connection, that she felt the spark he felt when he looked at her.

Today was the most direct conversation they'd had about what was happening, but he'd never tried to hide his interest, and he'd thought it was reciprocated. From the moment he'd met her, he'd gone out of his way to bump into her. She'd been pleasant. Cheerful. Smiling a lot. Had often had a sassy rebuttal to things he'd say. Had she just been being friendly? Polite?

After hearing her comment today, he had to wonder.

With her soulful brown eyes that held so much emotion, her silky chestnut hair she kept pulled up in a ponytail, pouty full lips, and almost fragile features, she'd caught his attention his first day at the hospital.

And held it.

He enjoyed their conversations, enjoyed sitting with her in the break room while she grabbed a quick lunch.

Although he'd yet to ask her out due to finishing up his move, settling into his new job and home, working three of the four weekends he'd been in Memphis and having to go home the previous weekend for his parents' anniversary, he'd planned to see if she was free for the upcoming weekend.

Not once had he questioned whether or not she'd say yes. He'd swear she was interested, that she enjoyed their light, fun conversations as much as he did.

Just the previous day, he'd asked her friend Rosalyn about her. Surprisingly, Rosalyn hadn't been able to tell him much about Carly's personal life. They'd worked together for five years, Carly didn't attend any of the hospital's social functions, rarely talked about family and never about anyone special.

None of their other co-workers had been able to tell him anything more.

He was a young healthy man who'd been used to an active social life since his divorce. Staying busy, active, was how he'd kept sane after Stephanie had left him. The fact his social life had been on hiatus from the move and job change was probably why he got so twisted up inside when he looked at Carly.

Although thinner than his usual taste, she was a beautiful woman, had a great sense of humor, and a quick smile.

When she smiled, his breath caught.

Rosalyn was right.

He had the hots for Carly.

Although he'd been in several relationships since his divorce, they'd all been light, fun, about mutual pleasure. From the moment he'd met her, Carly had tugged at something deep that made him question the meaningless relationships he moved in and out of with the ease of a broken heart that didn't allow anything more.

Memories of the past hit him, freezing him in place and making him question his interest in Carly.

Was she playing hard to get? Had he misread her? Or was there something more going on?

CHAPTER TWO

"SORRY I TOOK so long to bring your medicine," Carly apologized to the elderly man lying in the hospital bed.

Although partially dozed off, he wore a thick pair of glasses, along with oxygen tubing and a nasal cannula. He opened his eyes and stared in her direction, blankly at first, then with vague recognition.

Carly was used to that reaction. Wasn't it one she saw with increasing frequency from her mother?

Just as she did at home, Carly pasted on her brightest smile.

"I don't need medicine anyway," the man muttered grumpily and without making eye contact.

"Your medicine helps keep your heart in rhythm and will help get you out of this place and back home soon."

The man snorted. "I don't have a home."

Carly had been taking care of Mr. Taylor for three days, knew his personal history, and understood his frustrations that his family felt he could no longer live alone. With forgetting to eat and frequent falls, he couldn't.

"That's not what your daughter told me when she was visiting yesterday," Carly reminded him.

"She lied."

Carly handed him the plastic cup that held his pills. "You don't live with her?"

He thought a moment, then shook his head. He didn't say more, just took the medications.

"Is there anything else I can get you, Mr. Taylor?"

"A new body."

Carly smiled. She'd heard that many times over the five years she'd been a nurse.

"I wish I could," she admitted. She wished she could do a lot of things when it came to making someone well.

Especially with her mother's Parkinson's and dementia.

What she wouldn't do for there to be a cure to such horrific diseases that robbed one of their mind and body.

She checked his vitals, made sure his nurse-call button was within his reach, and left his room to check on another patient.

Mrs. Kim. A lovely little lady who'd had a surgically excised abscess on her chest. Due to the amount of infection and her weakened system, she'd been admitted for a few days for intravenous antibiotics to make sure the infection was knocked and to build up her strength.

Mrs. Kim's family had been taking turns staying during the evenings and night, but during the daytime her family worked and the woman was usually in her room alone.

Carly popped in frequently to check on her.

Most of the time the pleasant woman would be enthralled in whichever game show she was currently watching, but the vision that met Carly's eyes had her pausing in the doorway.

Looking distraught, Mrs. Kim was crying. Stone was at her bedside, holding her hand, offering comfort. Carly couldn't make out his exact words, but she could feel their soothing balm.

Could feel her own eyes watering in empathy at Mrs. Kim's distress.

Mrs. Kim grasped his hand in hers and was voicing her frustration over the wound that refused to heal in her chest, over how it was keeping her from her very busy life, and how she missed her two cats.

Whatever he said, Mrs. Kim weepily smiled, pulled his hand to her lips and smacked a kiss there.

"Thank you."

She said more, but Carly couldn't make out the words, just saw the woman's lips move and then Stone throw his head back and laugh.

A real laugh. One that reverberated through Carly. Made her long to share such a laugh with him.

How long had it been since she'd laughed like that? Carefree through and through? With all her worries set aside in the joy of the moment?

Since she'd felt any real, all-the-way-to-her-soul sense of joy?

No, that wasn't fair. She was happy, appreciative that she had her mother to go home to every day. It was what she wanted, what she'd choose given the choice. Every day was a blessing and to be cherished.

She did cherish life. She was *not* just going through the motions.

Thinking she'd come back later to check on Mrs. Kim, she turned to go, but the movement caught Stone's eye.

"Carly?"

Pasting a smile on her face, she stepped into the hospital room.

Ignoring Stone, she met her patient's gaze. "Hello, Mrs. Kim. I wanted to make sure you didn't need anything. I see you're in good hands."

Mrs. Kim's hand was locked between Stone's and the woman smiled. "Very."

"Is there anything you need?" She checked the woman's IV settings and vitals. Feeling Stone's gaze, she did her best to breathe normally, to function normally, and not make some total klutz move.

"Just to get better so I can go home."

"We're working on it," she promised, then wondered if she should have deferred to Stone.

She'd never gotten the impression he was one of those high-ego docs, but she'd only known him a month.

One month, four days.

Okay, so she was counting.

He didn't seem to mind her having answered for him. Possibly because he was too busy watching Carly's every move. As a doctor concerned about what his patient's nurse was doing? Maybe, but his expression was more inquisitive, as if he was trying to figure out what made her tick.

Good luck with that, she thought.

Actually, she was pretty dull. She worked and she took care of her mother. There wasn't time for anything more.

Just ask her ex-boyfriend.

"I'll be back in a little while to check on you," Carly promised, heading out the door.

When she reached for the handle, she couldn't resist glancing back. Her gaze collided with brilliant green.

His gaze holding hers, Stone smiled.

Something kicked in her chest.

Hard.

It might have been her heart skipping a beat or giving the strongest one in its twenty-seven-year history. Either way, she felt a little dizzy.

Carly's lips parted, because she should say something, right? The man moved her in ways she'd forgotten she could be moved.

Or had never known she could be moved.

But nothing came out of her mouth and she scurried out of the room, before she did something crazy.

Like admit that the problem with Stone was that he made her long to explore all the emotions sparking to life inside her.

But she wasn't free.

She needed to forget Stone.

Which was easier said than done since she saw the hospital's prized new surgeon every day she worked and every time she closed her eyes.

Stone wasn't wrong. He wasn't sure why Carly had said no to going to dinner with him, but she was as interested in him as he was her.

Desire had flashed in those eyes of hers.

Desire, longing, and so much more.

Which left him in a quandary.

He'd been rejected before, didn't have any desire to set himself up for another woman to walk away from him. But he needed to know why she'd said no when her eyes were begging him to sweep her off her feet.

"Hello," Carly called as she walked into her quiet house. The same house she'd grown up in. The same house she'd probably live in the rest of her life. "I'm home!"

She was. The small once white, but now faded, house was home, was where her heart and lots of wonderful memories were. Memories of better times when her mother had been well, full of spunk and energy, sharp-witted and capable of doing anything she wanted.

But those days were long gone.

For once Carly had gotten off work on time so hopefully her mother would still be awake, would hopefully be clear-minded, and not in the fog her memory often got enveloped by.

Joyce, her mother's nurse, came around the hallway corner and into the living room. "Busy day?"

Carly smiled at the sixty-something woman with gray hair she kept cut short and in loose, no-nonsense curls. A pair of thin gold-rimmed glasses sat on the bridge of her nose. She wore a Rolling Stones T-shirt with a big tongue on it and baggy, faded, rolled-up jeans that exposed slim ankles and flat white sandals.

Carly smiled. She and Joyce had an agreement the nurse wouldn't wear a uniform. She wanted her mother to feel she had a friend, not a medical professional. Joyce appreciated not having to don scrubs any more, too, as she'd done so for almost forty years prior to "retiring".

"They all are," Carly said, putting her handbag on the small dining table in one corner of the room. "But that's okay. I like to be busy."

"Which is a good thing because goodness knows you have enough on your plate for three people." Joyce tsked, shaking her head. "You need to slow down a little, and enjoy life before it passes you by."

"I'm fine." She was. Really, she was. So why did Stone's face pop into her mind and doubt fill her heart? She. Was. Fine. "There will be time for slowing down long before I'm ready." Which squeezed her insides and put things into proper perspective. "Speaking of which, how was Mom today?"

Joyce's expression tightened. "Not great. Getting her to eat is a major ordeal these days."

Carly winced. She knew from her own attempts to get her mother to eat. She seemed to have lost the will to live. "But she did eat?"

"She got her feeding tube meals, but by mouth." Joyce shook her head. "She just doesn't want anything."

Carly nodded, knowing the nurse would have done all she could to get as many nutrients into Carly's mother as possible.

"She struggled to communicate today," Joyce continued. "Not that she tried saying much, but, when she did, understanding her was more difficult than normal. And most of the day she called me Margaret."

Carly's grandmother, who'd passed away years ago.

Taking a deep breath, Carly nodded again.

"But in other news," the older woman began on a false

hopeful note, "Gerald texted to say he picked up ten lottery tickets and one was sure to be a winner this time."

Rubbing the back of her neck, massaging a knotted muscle, Carly smiled. Joyce's husband struggled with a lifelong gambling problem. These days, he limited himself to no more than ten tickets in each week's Powerball lotto.

"He says when he wins we're gonna put your momma somewhere real fine and move you out of this place."

Carly shook her head. "First off, I'd never let you do that and, second, I don't want to move. You know this is where Momma wants to be. I'll keep her here as long as I am physically and financially able."

Always. She'd always keep her mother at home. She hoped and prayed.

Joyce waved her hand. "You know what I meant."

She did. Joyce wanted to help, as did Gerald, to lighten Carly's burden. But Carly had this. Precariously, but she was making ends meet. She'd worry about sorting out all the tangles and knots later…hopefully, much later.

"Thank you for all you do. Nothing more is needed." She hoped it never was. "Just you taking care of Momma."

Joyce made another loud tsking sound. "I don't do nearly enough."

"You're here and that frees me to work without worrying about what kind of care Momma is getting. That's huge." As she thought about how different life would be without someone she trusted to care for her mother, Carly's eyes misted. "If I don't say thank you often enough, please know how grateful I am that I met you while doing my clinical rotation at the nursing home where you worked."

Joyce's eyes filled with love. "You say thank you about every other breath, and you know the feeling is mutual. Gerald and I love you and Audrey." The woman hugged Carly in a big bear hug, gathered her belongings, and got ready to leave. "Don't work too late into the night. You have to rest, too, you know."

Carly nodded. She worked a side job for an insurance company going through medical claims. The more claims she processed, the better her extra pay. While sitting next to her mother's bed, she'd work late tonight, processing as many claims as she accurately could.

"See you bright and early in the morning," she told the woman she truly didn't know what she'd do without.

Carly peeked in at her mother, saw she was resting, and went to the bathroom to grab a quick shower. When she'd finished and was dressed in old gray sweats and a baggy T-shirt, she checked her mother again, then went to make herself a sandwich before logging into the insurance company's website.

Work waited. It always did.

But when she went back into her mother's room, Audrey was awake.

"Hi, Mom. How was your day?" Some days her mother would answer. Some days her mother just stared blankly.

"S-same a-as a-always-s." Although slurred, her mother answered, which made Carly's heart swell. Did she know who Carly was today?

"Mine, too. Busy, busy, busy. Some of my patients are the same ones I mentioned to you last night, but I did have a couple of new ones." Carly never gave names or identifying information, but chatted about her patients. She tried to make her stories interesting, to give her mother a link to the outside world as often as she could.

Audrey rarely left the house these days. When she did it was usually to go to a doctor's appointment.

Before Carly knew it she was telling her mother about walking in on the new surgeon and how he'd been holding his patient's hand, comforting her.

"I-i-is h-he h-h-handsome?"

"Gorgeous," she admitted. "He's also very kind and funny. The man makes me smile."

Realizing she was going on too much about Stone, she glanced at her mother.

Her mother who was staring oddly at her. "Y-you l-like h-him?"

Oops. Not the first time today she'd been asked that.

But, unlike at the hospital, to her mother, she nodded. "He seems like a great guy."

"Y-you sh-should g-go out with h-him."

Her mother knew her. If she thought Carly was Margaret, she'd be scolding rather than encouraging her mother to cheat on her father.

"Mom, he's a doctor. I'm a nurse. How cliché can you get?" She tried to keep her voice teasing and fun and similar to conversations they might have had during Carly's teenaged and college years when Carly had dated, when she'd been wrapped up in Tony and thought he was her forever person. "Besides, Stone's way out of my league."

"Wh-why?"

"Because he's such a great catch."

"S-so a-are y-you."

"You, my dearest mother, are the tiniest bit biased." Carly stood, bent over and kissed her mother's cheek. While her mother was with her, really with her, Carly wanted to milk the moment for every precious second. "Truly, he's out of my league. Even if he wasn't, it would never work."

"Be-because of m-me?"

"Of course not," Carly gasped. Never would she want her mother to think such a thing, never would she want her feeling guilt over Carly taking care of her to the exclusion of everything else. It was a privilege to take care of her mother. One Carly treasured and had never thought twice about...until Stone.

Darn him. That he made her discontent with the status quo was enough that she should dislike him.

"To-Tony," her mother began.

Despite the slight thrill that her mother's memory was

working at the moment, Carly stopped her. "Tony was an idiot and I was lucky to be rid of him."

She was. Any man who couldn't understand that Carly had to take care of her mother, that her mother came first, well, he needed to hit the road. She'd needed Tony's support; instead, he'd resented everything about Audrey.

"Tony has nothing to do with why Stone and I would never work. He and I are just not physically or economically compatible. That's all."

"I-if h-he th-thinks that then y-you are b-better off wi-without h-him."

"Exactly." Before her mother could talk more about Tony or Stone—why on earth had Carly mentioned him?—Carly launched into a tale about another patient, exaggerating to make the recounting more entertaining.

Because tonight her mother looked at her and saw her daughter. Sometimes that wasn't the case.

Sometimes it was all Carly could do not to cry.

Sometimes she did cry.

But not tonight. Tonight she smiled and enjoyed talking to the weak woman lying in the hospital bed that took up a good portion of the bedroom.

Tonight her mother was mentally her mother.

"Any regrets?"

Having just stepped out of a patient room, Carly spun toward the sound of Stone's voice near her ear and almost collided with him.

"About what?" she asked, stepping back because of his close proximity. He wore dark navy scrubs that made his green eyes pop.

She glanced up and down the empty hospital hallway. Although the nurses' station was within view, no one was paying them the slightest attention.

"Not going to dinner with me last night." His voice teased, but his eyes asked real questions.

"Not a single one." The truth. She prized the evening she'd spent with her mother until she'd dozed off and Carly had worked on insurance claims late into the early morning hours.

Stone's sigh was so dramatic someone should give him an award. "Pity."

Despite knowing the best thing was to walk away, to not encourage him in any shape, form, or fashion, she couldn't resist asking, "Why's that?"

His gaze locked with hers, sparkled like an emerald sea. "We'd have had a good time."

She rolled her eyes. "Spoken like a true man."

"Meaning?"

"Men automatically think you getting to spend time with them means you'll have a good time." Tony had thought that. "That's not always the case, you know."

His grin was quick. "We should test that theory."

Step away, Carly. Don't get pulled in by his charm.

"By?" she asked, unable to follow her own advice, and wondering how long they could linger in the hallway prior to someone taking notice.

"Going to dinner with me tonight."

Her gaze met his. "I've already told you no to going to dinner tonight."

"That was yesterday. Today's a new day."

"My answer hasn't changed."

"It should."

Rosalyn stepped out of a patient room, glanced toward Carly and Stone, and stopped to stare.

"That's a matter of opinion," Carly quipped.

Obviously, Rosalyn's opinion ran more along the lines of Stone's. Grinning big, she gave a thumb up.

"Your opinion is that you should deprive yourself of dinner with me?"

"Deprive myself?" Carly snorted, then shook her head at Rosalyn. "I'll survive just fine if we never go to dinner."

Turning, Stone shot a grin at Rosalyn, who smiled back, then headed toward the nurses' station.

"You won't know what you're missing."

Shifting her weight, Carly squinted at him. "Is that supposed to bother me?"

His eyes flashed somewhere between serious and teasing. "It should."

"Why?"

"Because there's something between you and I."

Her breath caught. She felt it. He felt it. Thoughts of her mother were all that kept her from throwing herself at the mercy of whatever he wanted. She had no time for a relationship, no energy for a relationship. Everything she had, and more, was already claimed.

"You're wrong." She smiled tightly. "There's nothing I want from you."

"Why don't I believe you?"

Because I'm a horrible liar and usually pride myself on being a person who tells the truth, but with you...

She didn't want his pity. Or his rejection if he felt the same as Tony had.

"I don't know," she replied, not meeting his eyes. "Why don't you?"

"Because you're not telling the truth."

She hadn't expected him to call her bluff, and her gaze shot to his. "How dare you say such a thing?"

"Because it's true."

She lifted her chin in indignation, partly feigned, partly real, at his arrogance. "So your word gets taken as the truth, but not mine?"

"In this case, yes."

"What an ego you have, Dr. Parker."

"Stating facts doesn't make me egotistical."

Carly put her hands on her hips and glared at him with

the sternest look she could muster. Not an easy thing to do when he was grinning at her with his brilliant smile and twinkling eyes.

"Is there a point to this conversation?"

"Just enjoying your company." His tone was teasing, but the glint in his eyes said he told the truth.

If she were honest, she'd admit she was enjoying his company, too. Which was ridiculous considering what their actual words were. Was she really that desperate for any scrap of his attention?

"I've work to do." She glanced down the hallway and caught Rosalyn and a nurse's aide watching them.

"Am I interfering with your work, Carly?"

"Yes." Carly's head hurt. Or maybe it was her heart.

"How so?"

"You're distracting me."

His eyes danced. "You're admitting you find me distracting? Finally, we're getting somewhere."

She bit the inside of her lower lip, then shook her head. "Dr. Parker, I shouldn't be having lengthy personal conversations while on the clock."

"Which is why you should go to dinner with me tonight. We could have lengthy personal conversations to our hearts' content."

She wanted to. She wanted to say yes, go to dinner with him, and stare into his eyes all evening. Longer.

But, even if she could, how unfair would that be to him? Very. To lead him, or anyone, on was wrong.

She should tell him, should apologize for smiling when he sat with her at break, for laughing at his corny jokes, for looking at him and longing for things outside her grasp.

But she couldn't find the words, so she hurried away, dodging into a patient room to avoid both the man she could feel watching her and her two co-workers anxiously waiting to question her.

She didn't think of herself as a woman who ran from her problems. But, at the moment, running from temptation, and the questioning thereof, seemed the best course of action.

CHAPTER THREE

"CAN I HELP you with that?"

Carly peeped at Stone from over the top of the box she carried through the hospital corridor. He'd changed out of his navy scrubs into his own clothes, black trousers and a green polo shirt that perfectly matched the color of his eyes. She fought sighing in appreciation. The man should be in movies, not a hospital operating room.

"I've got it," she assured him. "Thanks anyway."

Ignore him and maybe he'll go away. Not likely, but maybe.

"That box is bigger than you are."

The sturdy box was more bulky than heavy. Inside were expired medical supplies the hospital couldn't use. Carly had gotten clearance from upper management to take the expired supplies home with her. No one at the hospital knew about her mother, but they did know she sat with someone on her days off work.

There might not be a thing she could use. But Carly would go through the box, pull out what she could use, and take the rest to a free health clinic for the uninsured that could hopefully make use of the items.

"You look like it's all you can do to keep steady. Quit being stubborn and let me help you, Carly," Stone insisted, his voice sounding off a little.

He had a point. Plus, Carly's fingers ached from gripping the box so hard and she was curious why his voice wavered. "Fine."

He took the box from her with an ease indicating it weighed no more than a feather, then beamed as if he'd done something amazingly chivalrous. Whatever had caused the waver, he was all smiles now.

"Lead the way."

As in to her car.

She didn't want Stone to see her reliable, but old sedan. Whereas most people didn't notice the little details in Carly's life that hinted things might not be fairy tales and roses, that sharp mind of his would question things she didn't want questioned.

She didn't want him making her question things.

Pushing the hospital door open and holding it for him, she sighed. "Of all the people who offered to help, it would have to be you."

"If I didn't know better, I'd think you didn't like me."

"I don't know you well enough to like or dislike you," she said as she made sure the hospital door completely closed. "I only know you from the hospital and what little interaction we've had here."

"I keep trying to correct that."

"You want me to know you well enough to dislike you?" She pretended to misunderstand in hopes of redirecting the conversation. Besides, he deserved a little taking down.

Rather than look offended, he laughed. "I'm hoping you'll swing the other way and like me."

Fighting a smile, she narrowed her gaze at him. "But you're admitting there is a distinct possibility I won't?"

"It's not been a big problem, but you wouldn't be the first." He cut his eyes toward her. "For the record, I'd prefer you like me."

"Noted," she said, keeping a step ahead of him as they crossed the employee parking lot.

"Go to dinner with me, Carly."

He was asking her again. How could something be so unbelievably dreamy and such a nightmare at the same time?

"I can't." Part of her wanted to. Part of her wanted to grab her box and run.

Despite how she'd hightailed it from him earlier, she didn't run from her problems. She dealt with them head on and chin up.

Just as she had with Rosalyn and the nurse's aide's teasing questions about Stone.

"Because?" he prompted.

Because she had to relieve Joyce. The retired nurse was wonderful, never complained if Carly worked overtime, but, otherwise, Carly always came straight home.

"Are you involved with a married man?"

Almost tripping, eyes wide, Carly spun toward Stone. "What? Are you crazy? Of course not. What would make you think that?"

His gaze, not so twinkly at the moment, stared into her eyes. "No one knows anything about your private life, yet you say you're busy."

She glared for real. "Because I'm not interested in you that means I must be sneaking around with a married man?" She rolled her eyes. "Get over yourself, Dr. Parker."

He winced. "That's not what I meant."

"It's what you implied and I don't appreciate it." Was that what he'd taken away from the short bits of time they'd spent together? That she was a woman who would mess around with a man who'd vowed himself to another woman?

"I'm sorry. That's not what I meant to imply."

Hanging onto her anger proved difficult when his apology was full of sincerity. Frustrated with herself, she put her hands on her hips. "Then say what you mean."

He shifted the box. "Regardless of what I say, I upset you."

"You should take the hint and not say anything, then."

"What's the fun in that?"

"What's the fun in upsetting me?" she tossed back and took off toward her car in a fast walk.

"You're right," Stone said from right behind her. "I take no pleasure in upsetting you. The truth is I want to do the opposite."

"You want to take pleasure in upsetting me?" She pretended to misunderstand, again. She felt contrary and purposely misunderstanding gave her a little reprieve. Asking if she was seeing a married man! The nerve. "Thanks, but no, thanks."

Okay, she might be latching onto that to throw a wall between them. She needed whatever shield she could find to protect her from the charm he exuded.

Digging her key out of her pocket, Carly unlocked her old economy sedan, then hit the button on the car-door panel to unlock the back doors. She opened the backseat door, tugging a little extra hard where the door often stuck, then stepped back for Stone to put the box onto the seat.

He made sure the box wasn't going anywhere if she slammed on her brakes or took a curve a little fast, then faced her. "Is it me, then, or men in general?"

"Is your ego so big that you just can't fathom I'm not interested?"

He closed the car door and moved to where he stood right in Carly's personal space. "My ego isn't that big and if it had been, you'd have corrected that."

Ouch.

"What I'd like," he continued, "is to know why you say you aren't interested when I'd put money on the fact you are."

Hands digging into her hips, she glared. "You'd lose your money."

"Would I?" His question was gentle rather than mocking. "I'm not sure what changed yesterday, Carly. I'm not blind. I've seen how you look at me. It's the same way I look at you. With interest. If my delay in asking you out is the problem, know it wasn't from lack of interest. On the days I haven't worked, I've been traveling back and forth from Atlanta to settle up everything with my move."

Any spunk Carly had left her like a deflating balloon.

Any woman would be flattered at Stone's attention. If his ego had been huge, it would be with good reason.

And she was flattered by his attention.

But his attention was a distraction she didn't need because she had to stay focused. Losing focus could mean everything falling apart and she couldn't allow that to happen.

Plus, how could she in good conscience involve any man in her crazy life? Just look at how Tony had balked and her mother hadn't been nearly as needful at that time.

She closed her eyes. "It would be simpler if you'd move on and forget whatever interest you have in me."

"Do you remember when we first met?"

Stone's question caught her off guard. Her eyes popped open and she stared at him.

"You were coming out of the medical supply room and bumped into me," he continued, his gaze searching hers. "You almost fell over yourself apologizing." A soft smile played on his lips. "I thought you were the prettiest thing I'd seen in a long time."

Vanities were not something Carly had the time or money to indulge in. She kept her hair in a no-maintenance style of long and natural to where she could pull it up and not bother with highlights or salons. She hadn't worn make-up since college. Money was too tight for such frivolities. His calling her the prettiest thing stirred up a thousand butterflies in her belly.

"I think that right now."

His words set every butterfly into fluttery flight. Oh, my. Carly gulped.

"You must have had your eyes closed a long time, then." She fought to keep from putting her hand over her stomach.

Studying her, he shook his head. "You were in these same blue scrubs, but had on different shoes. Your laces were bright orange rather than neon green."

He remembered what she'd been wearing when they first met? That her shoe laces had been a different color?

"You are a lovely woman, Carly."

To which she could only say, "Thank you."

Embarrassed, feeling a little shaky at the knees, Carly glanced around the employee parking lot and caught sight of a co-worker curiously looking her way, the nurse's aide who'd been with Rosalyn earlier.

The woman called out, "Goodnight."

Carly waved and wished her a good evening as well, then frowned at the man still standing too close.

"She's a wonderful person, but does tend to gossip. No doubt, everyone will know you were at my car with me."

"Then we should give them something to talk about." The eye-twinkle was back.

Horrified, Carly shook her head. "No, we shouldn't."

She needed her job, couldn't risk anything creating waves at her place of employment. Not even the temptation in Stone's eyes.

He sighed and raked his fingers through his hair. "You're right. Sorry. I seem to have a one-track mind where you're concerned. Give me your address. I'll follow you home and carry the box inside."

"Not going to happen." No way would she be able to explain to Joyce why a handsome doctor had followed her home. Carrying a heavy box in wouldn't begin to satisfy the protective older woman's curiosity.

As for Stone's one-track mind, why was her body heating up at the possibilities of what he'd meant?

"Are you capable of saying yes to anything I suggest?"

Yeah, she was being ornery. For her own safety and sanity. His, too.

"Probably not," she admitted, giving a wry smile.

"I'm a pretty straightforward guy. I'd like to date you, Carly. I've been trying to get to know you and thought we were until yesterday. If my overhearing your conversation with Rosalyn upset you that much, I truly am sorry." His tone was appropriately repentant. "I want to take you out, talk with you, dine with you away from the hospital, and eventually kiss those lips of yours that I find myself thinking about way too often."

Insides shaking, heart pulled into a tug-of-war between need and want and guilt, Carly closed her eyes. "I can't do this."

"You can't talk to me?"

"I can't hear you say those things," she clarified, not opening her eyes. In a tug-of-war of its own, her mind raced between logic and emotion and loyalty to her mother.

Stone wanted to date her. Stone wanted to *kiss* her. She'd not been kissed in so long. Not since Tony.

Suddenly the need to be kissed, to feel like a woman, to feel alive and wanted and young, burst free and filled every cell of her being to overflowing.

Which was what made Stone so very dangerous to all she held dear.

He could make a total disaster of her life.

"Because?"

Had his voice been closer? She thought so, but she didn't open her eyes to check. She couldn't look, couldn't see whatever was in his magnificent green eyes.

Stone tempted. Tempted her to want things she shouldn't want.

Couldn't want.

Couldn't have.

Which didn't seem to matter because she was a woman with normal urges and he made all those urges come on full force whether she wanted them to or not.

Probably the rest of her life she'd look back and wish

circumstances had presented her with the option to throw caution to the wind with Stone Parker.

To forget the pain of Tony turning his back on her.

To embrace all the warmth and urges Stone stirred.

Because she'd like him to kiss her. Had not been able to stop the late-night thoughts about what it would feel like to be kissed by him.

Now, he'd said he wanted to kiss her.

How was she ever supposed to get him out of her head when he'd verbalized things she'd fantasized?

"Carly?"

His voice was so close, her name whispered against her cheek.

"Hmm?"

"Open your eyes."

She bit the inside of her lower lip. "I can't."

"There's a lot of things you say you can't do, lady."

"Exactly. You should run."

"I don't believe there's anything you can't do."

He was definitely closer. She'd swear she just felt his breath tickle her ear.

"For the record," he continued, "I'm not going anywhere."

The brevity of his words dug in deep, breaking through barriers that were best left alone.

"Not unless you tell me to," he clarified. "Then I will leave you alone, because I'm not some psycho stalker, just a man wanting to date a beautiful woman."

Tell him to go away.

Tell him sticking around is futile.

Tell him...

Stone's lips brushed against her hairline, near her ear. Soft, gentle, tentative. Not a sexual kiss, but one full of longing and question and space. Space that gave her control of what happened next.

Carly's eyes shot open, stared into his eyes, and she wondered at what she saw there.

Desire, confusion, so much she couldn't label.

"Tell me you aren't curious, Carly. Tell me I'm crazy when I look in your eyes and see a kindred desire. Tell me to put you in your car, watch you drive away, never think of you again, and I'll try to do just that."

Tell him.

Not to do so would be selfish.

Self-destructive.

But her lips refused to cooperate so she said nothing.

"Tell me what you want, Carly."

She didn't know what she wanted.

Not true. She wanted him to do exactly what he'd said he wanted to do. She wanted him to kiss her.

Crazy.

She wasn't free to have a relationship. To pull some unsuspecting man into her chaotic life wouldn't be fair.

Plus, with two jobs and her mother, she barely slept as it was. Where would she fit in a relationship?

She opened her mouth, determined to tell him she only wanted a professional relationship, that he needed to forget about her and whatever it was he thought he'd seen when she looked at him.

So why did she hear her address spill from her lips?

She was crazy. She couldn't let him into her house, couldn't let Joyce or her mother hear his voice.

Surprise lit in his eyes, then, with a smile, he nodded. "I'll follow you home and carry in the box."

What had she done?

And why?

Because she wanted to know what it felt like to kiss Stone?

It wasn't as if she were actually going to kiss him.

Only in her deepest darkest late-night fantasies and even

then she barely gave her mind license to imagine Stone's lips against hers.

She'd made a horrible mistake by giving him her address. Just what did he think it had meant? If he was thinking he was staying the night, he was going to be in for a rude awakening when he realized an invalid woman also lived at Carly's address.

Carly got into her car, leaned forward, and rested her forehead against the steering wheel.

Clearly, she'd lost her mind.

Or maybe, because she hadn't been able to verbalize the reasons why they could never be, her subconscious had taken control, and was going to confront Stone with the harsh reality of why he needed to forget her.

That harsh reality had certainly scared off the last man Carly had brought home.

Had Carly given Stone a bogus address?

If she had, Stone couldn't say he'd be surprised.

He hoped she hadn't, but had to wonder. She'd thrown it out at a point where the last thing he'd expected was an invitation to her home.

She hadn't technically invited him to her house, but hadn't that been what giving her address to him had essentially been?

As he'd only moved to Memphis a month before and was still learning the city, he programmed the details into his GPS and noted she only lived six minutes from the hospital and about fifteen from him as he lived over the bridge on Mud Island.

At least, he'd know pretty quickly if she'd told him the truth. And if she hadn't?

Well, that should tell him that she wanted him to leave her alone.

Only she didn't want that. He knew she didn't.

She hadn't even been able to say the words.

He'd flirted with her at the hospital on more than one occasion. She'd flirted back. Not overtly, but her smiles and sassy eye flashes and little laughs at his jokes had all been leading up to something. What had happened yesterday that had her scurrying back?

No matter how many times he replayed the conversation, he couldn't fathom what had put her on the defensive.

Not quite liking the looks of the run-down neighborhood and having been warned not to go wandering around parts of Memphis he was unfamiliar with, Stone questioned again if Carly had given him a made-up address. He turned onto her street, and, best as he could tell, the houses on the street were small, older, but decently cared for.

His GPS told him he'd arrived at his destination and he pulled up his SUV outside a small once-white frame house that even in the dark he could tell needed some major TLC. Much more so than the surrounding homes.

That surprised him.

Carly was meticulous in her care of patients and all that she did at her job. To ignore upkeep on her home didn't fit what he believed about her. He could be wrong, but he struggled to wrap his mind around the neglect that registered.

He wouldn't have guessed her to live in the house of obvious worst repair on her street.

Then again, maybe she rented the place and her landlord was the slacker.

As a nurse, she made a decent salary to where she could afford to move if she was renting and things weren't up to par. If she had some long-term lease that had her trapped in the run-down house, maybe he could call on a lawyer friend to get her into something better maintained.

He would help her find another place.

A place closer to his on Mud Island.

There was another car, a much newer sedan, parked in the drive beside hers. Did she have a roommate?

She must have just pulled into the short gravel driveway right before him as when he turned off the SUV's engine and opened his door, Carly got out of her car.

"You really didn't need to do this," she said immediately, before he could ask about the other car. "Yes, it's bulky, but I would have gotten the box inside without any problems. I was doing just fine before you came to my rescue."

"No need to risk hurting your back when you have me."

Whether she wanted him or not, he planned to help Carly because he suspected more was going on than met the eye with the woman who'd captured his imagination.

CHAPTER FOUR

STONE WAS AT Carly's house.

Now that he was there, what was Carly supposed to do with him?

Let him carry the box to her porch and send him away?

It was what she wanted to do, what she was tempted to do.

Somehow she didn't think he would agree to it though. He had that "let me be your knight in shining armor" look that she'd seen in the movies her mother enjoyed watching, but that Carly had never seen in real life.

Until now.

If Stone went inside, it was quite possible her mother would be asleep and Carly could avoid that explanation. But Joyce would be there and ready to head to her home to spend the evening with her husband.

Joyce seeing Stone would raise questions. From Joyce, but perhaps more so from Stone.

Maybe she could have him set the box just inside the doorway and get him back outside prior to Joyce realizing they were there. Before Stone realized there was someone else in the house.

Unlikely, but she could try.

Or she could just tell Stone everything.

Which made her stomach hurt.

She didn't want him to feel sorry for her or feel obligated to offer help. The past had taught her people might think they wanted to help, but most only offered idle words.

She had this. She could take care of her mother.

She could, she was, and she would.

Or was it that she was afraid he'd pull a Tony?

Wasn't that what she actually needed him to do? What would be best for her and Stone?

So, why was she hesitating?

"It's no problem," Stone assured her, pulling Carly back to their conversation as he lifted the box out of her backseat.

"Thank you." She shut the car door then moved ahead of him to unlock her front door.

She turned, wondering if Stone would be agreeable to drop the box in the foyer and leave.

Maybe she was a runner after all, because if she could escape this moment, her tennis shoes would be getting a desperately needed workout.

Stone carried the box, stopped just inside the doorway and asked, "Where would you like me to put this?"

She pointed to a small wooden bench that had once upon a time belonged to her long-gone grandparents. "Right there is fine."

He set the box down. "What's in this thing, anyway?"

"Stolen goods from the hospital."

His eyes narrowed.

Nerves still shaking up her insides, Carly grinned. "Gotcha."

His lips twitched. "Maybe a little."

"It's expired hospital supplies that were going to be tossed," she admitted, wondering if she was strong enough to toss him out the front door before Joyce saw him. The nurse must have been tied up with Audrey or she'd have already greeted Carly.

Stone glanced toward the box. "What do you do with the supplies?"

She shrugged. Best to stick with the truth. "Use what I

can and donate the rest. Let's go back outside." *Please.* "I think I left something in the car."

"Oh." He turned toward the front door, but they were too late.

"I thought I heard voices in here," Joyce said, entering the room, then stopping when she spotted Stone.

Carly's stomach dropped.

Startled, Stone glanced toward Carly, then back at the woman who was gawking at him as if she didn't believe her eyes. She must not have because she was adjusting her glasses as if they'd stopped working.

Quickly recovering, Stone stuck out his hand. "Stone Parker." He flashed his amazing smile. "I work with Carly."

"You're a nurse?" Joyce's gaze went back and forth between them.

Carly inwardly cringed at the questions in the older woman's eyes. Joyce was trying to figure out who Stone was and why he was there. Maybe she even thought he was trying to replace her as Audrey's sitter. As if.

"He's a doctor," Carly clarified to make sure there was no doubt Joyce's job was not in jeopardy. Far from it. Carly needed Joyce every moment she could afford her.

"You're a doctor?" Joyce asked, sounding a bit incredulous. "Sign me up for some healthcare. I think I'm way past due for my physical."

Heat infused Carly's cheeks at Joyce's off-color remark.

Stone's smile dug his dimples deep into his cheeks. He was probably used to such comments from women of all ages. "I'll have to give you my card so you can schedule an appointment."

Joyce's eyes twinkled. "You do that."

"Nice shirt, by the way."

Joyce looked down at the vintage Kiss T-shirt she wore with the four band members in full make-up and leather garb framed in a fiery circle. "Thanks. My husband and I were music buffs in our younger years." She glanced over the gold rim of her glasses. "I have quite the collection."

"Stone helped me carry in a box of supplies the hospital was getting rid of," Carly said, trying to explain his presence.

Joyce nodded toward the box. "I see that."

"But he has to go now," Carly added, not meeting Stone's eyes but staring at his forehead instead.

His brows veed. "I do?"

"Yes, you do."

Disappointment clouding his expression, he frowned. "Oh."

"Unless you'd like to stay for dinner," Joyce offered, obviously thinking she needed to keep Stone there. "I could whip something up."

Ha. Carly would like to know what the woman could whip together. She'd not been to the grocery store that week and wouldn't for another two days. Not until after payday. Even then, it would be meager shopping as her mother's neurologist had started her on a new medication that month hoping to better control her tremors. The new medicine hadn't been covered by insurance and Carly had dipped into what little she had put back for a rainy day. If the medicine helped her mother, it was worth whatever the cost.

"Since I couldn't convince Carly to go to dinner to keep me from dining alone, dinner here would be great."

Carly shot him a dirty look. That was a low blow, she mentally willed him to hear.

"Carly wouldn't go to dinner with you?" Joyce sent her an "Are you crazy?" look. "Why not?"

"You know why not."

Please don't say anything about Momma. Please. I don't want Stone involved.

"I could've stayed late. I wouldn't have minded."

How tacky did it sound to say she couldn't afford her to stay late? Especially not this month.

"I have to ask you often enough when I'm stuck behind at work," she reminded her. "I don't expect you to work late here so I can go to dinner with a new co-worker. That wouldn't be fair."

"Work?" Stone asked, obviously confused.

"What's not fair is you not going to eat dinner with this young man. I insist you go."

Although confused and obviously enjoying Joyce taking his side, Stone looked as if he was trying to connect all the dots. Hoping he wouldn't was futile.

Carly was exhausted by it all. Her long work day. Stone and all the crazy emotions he made her feel. Her mother's illness. Joyce and her motherly concern that Carly wasn't having the life she deserved.

Who got the life they deserved?

Not many. Maybe not anyone.

Overall, Carly was content with life. She had enough to pay the bills—barely—and she had her mother. That was all that mattered.

"You should listen to your mother."

Stone thought Joyce was her mother?

"Joyce isn't my mother, or even blood kin, although I do love her as if she is family." Carly took a deep breath. "My mother has late stage Parkinson's disease with dementia and requires full-time care. Joyce stays with Momma while I am at work."

"And would have been glad to stay this evening so you could go to dinner," Joyce jumped in to say. "You need to get out more. You're way too young to spend all your free time locked away inside this house."

Advice Joyce gave several times every week, but that didn't change a thing. Carly chose to live her life by taking care of her mother. Her only regret was that her mother was so ill.

Bracing herself for what she might see, Carly brought

her gaze to Stone's face, expecting the worst, probably because of Tony.

"I agree with Joyce." His gaze searched hers, a million questions shining in the green depths. Most of which centered around, "Why didn't you tell me about your mother?"

Carly bit the inside of her cheek.

"You are way too young, and beautiful," he added, his eyes not wavering from hers, "to be locked away. For whatever it's worth, I'm sorry about your mother."

His empathy was something Carly didn't want. Not that she preferred him to be cold or callous, just that…well, she didn't want his pity.

Wasn't that part of why she kept her private life private? That, and she wanted to just be happy at work without anyone judging her for doing so when her mother was so ill. Being down and out wouldn't change her mother's illness, so Carly chose to pretend life was grand when she was at the hospital. She could smile and laugh and not feel judged for feeling joy. It helped her feel…normal.

"It's not as if I feel locked away." She didn't. She felt blessed to take care of her mother, to have the time with her that she did. "This is my home. I like it here."

She'd grown up within these walls, had once played in the small backyard. Her, her mother, and her grandparents. She'd had a carefree childhood, not understanding how poor they were or how hard her mother worked to make ends meet after her grandparents had died. Her mother had been diagnosed with Parkinson's Carly's senior year of high school, but that hadn't stopped her from working or living her life. Not initially.

Carly had moved away for college, but when, during Carly's senior year at university, her mother's disease had progressed, causing her to leave her job, Carly had moved home. She'd had to. Her mother had needed help with expenses as she'd been on the verge of losing the house to her mortgage company.

Through endless hours of hard work, Carly had saved the house, taken over her mother's limited finances, and worked as much overtime at her waitressing job as she could to make headway on the enormous burden of medical bills, the expenses of keeping up a house, and all the other bills that had seemed to hit her from every direction. Plus, she'd maintained her grades, gone to clinicals, and somehow found time to study for her nursing board examination.

That had been just over five years ago. Although Carly's income had jumped upon graduation, her mother's health had continued to deteriorate and her expenses had skyrocketed. Audrey had been unable to stay home alone for the past three years and been mostly bedridden for the past year. Although taking a huge chunk of Carly's income, Joyce had been a life-saver and was worth every penny.

To keep treading water and making a little progress from time to time, Carly worked her hospital job, worked from home reviewing the claims for a large insurance company, cared for her mother, and slept whenever she could squeeze in a few hours. Things were tight and Carly often felt she was barely managing to juggle all the bills, but it could be worse. She could be sinking rather than treading the surface.

Or even worse, she could not have her mother.

She wouldn't complain.

"Of course, you do, dear," Joyce assured her, coming over and giving Carly a quick hug. When she pulled back, she gave Carly that motherly look that made her feel as if she were five rather than a grown woman. "I'll stay with Audrey and you go have a nice meal."

Five or twenty-seven, Carly started to protest.

"I don't have plans tonight. Gerald has his bowling league and won't be home until late," Joyce countered before Carly could get started. "I'll be going home to an empty house, so I'd gladly stay for free."

Joyce had offered to come in to help Carly on numerous occasions, offering not to charge anything for her time. She truly had become like family. Still, Carly had hoped she'd never have to take the woman up on her offer. She didn't want handouts.

She shook her head. "I can't ask you to do that. You already do too much."

"You didn't ask. I offered." Joyce glanced toward Stone, gave him an appreciative once-over. "Actually, I insist. Go relax for an hour or so, Carly. I'd just gotten your mother changed as you were getting home. She fell asleep as I redressed her. She isn't likely to wake any time soon. I can heat some soup and catch the news here just as easily as I can at home. Go."

Carly bit the inside of her cheek. She couldn't say yes, could she? The expression on Joyce's face said the woman wasn't leaving without an argument. "You're sure you don't mind?"

"Positive."

"We could bring back dessert," Stone offered, his gaze focused on Carly, except to flash a quick smile to the older woman.

Joyce smiled at him in a way that made Carly wonder if the woman was seeing wedding bells and a solution to Carly's financial woes, just in case Gerald's lottery numbers failed to produce miracles again this week.

"I like your fellow already, Carly. He knows the way to a woman's heart. Dessert."

Carly started to correct Joyce, to tell her that Stone was not her fellow, but she wouldn't believe her, so what was the point?

Carly turned toward Stone. "Fine. If you'll give me fifteen minutes to check my mother, change out of my uniform and freshen up, I'll go to dinner."

"Take all the time you need. In case you haven't figured it out, I'm not going anywhere."

Telling her heart not to believe him, that he didn't know what he was saying, Carly stepped into her mother's bedroom.

The rhythmic rise and fall of her mother's chest was reassuring. Joyce was right. Her mother wasn't likely to wake any time soon. Generally, Carly came home, ate leftovers or something cheap she could rustle up, then logged in remotely to the insurance company and worked until whatever time her mother woke. Generally, she woke around midnight, was awake for about an hour, and then was out again for the rest of the night. Carly usually headed to bed at whatever time her mother dozed back off.

Last night had been a blessing that her mother had been awake, aware, and communicative. A rare treat.

With Joyce at the house, Carly could go to dinner. She had several hours' worth of insurance claims to go through, but she could do that when she got back and just not sleep as much. Who needed sleep, right?

Besides, she owed Stone an explanation, to verbalize that at least now he knew why a relationship between them was impossible.

Which she could do right now without their going to dinner. So why wasn't she?

Right or wrong, she was going to dinner with the man she'd fallen asleep and dreamed of the night before.

God help her.

"Is your mother why you said no to going out with me, Carly?" Stone asked the moment they got into his SUV.

His high-end fancy SUV with leather seats and more gadgets than a spaceship.

"There goes your ego talking again," she said flippantly, thinking that just the contrast in their vehicles should warn she shouldn't be with him.

They were as different as day and night.

"You didn't answer my question."

"Sure, I did," she countered, buckling her seat belt over the black trousers and plain rust-colored blouse she'd pulled from the back of her closet. She'd half expected the car to automatically buckle her in.

"Pride isn't why I'm asking," he assured her, pushing a button on the dash and starting the vehicle.

But maybe pride was why she felt so inadequate sitting in his "all the bells and whistles" SUV. Ugh. She didn't like what that said about her.

He punched in some letters she didn't catch on the GPS on his dashboard. He made sure there weren't any cars coming, then pulled away from her house and onto the street.

"There's lots of reasons why I've said no."

"Such as?" He turned the car down a street, then made another quick turn, following the directions from the car's navigation system.

Carly stared out the window, realized they were headed toward downtown.

"My life is full," she finally answered.

"Not in a good way."

Walls shot up and she glared across the car. "That's a matter of opinion. For the record, I wouldn't change it."

Because the only way her life was going to get easier was if something happened to her mother. God forbid. Her mother was everything.

"I understand that…" Stone's tone softened as he pulled the car into a restaurant parking lot "…but it is unfortunate you live as if you're a hermit."

Looking around at his restaurant pick, she realized he'd chosen one she'd mentioned during one of their lunches.

Julio's. Of all the ones he could have picked, why this one? Totally her fault. She'd been the one to mention Julio's.

"Don't pay any attention to what Joyce said." Or to what she said, because Carly couldn't believe they were at the restaurant where she'd worked during high school and university. "I think she may just be trying to scope out more work hours."

Guilt slammed her for suggesting such a falsehood. Joyce wasn't doing any such thing. Ugh.

He turned the ignition off and turned toward her. "I didn't get that impression."

Because he was astute and there hadn't been any reason for him to get that impression because Joyce was an angel.

Carly reached for the door handle. "Let it go. It's my choice, Stone, one I am happy to make."

After all, her mother had always worked hard, had done everything she could to be there for Carly, to provide for her physically and emotionally. All without help from Carly's father. Carly had no complaints.

She'd had a great childhood where she'd been loved and had loved. That was more than many people ever had.

So what if her twenties had been heavily laden thus far? If Carly was lucky that load would be carried into her thirties, her forties even.

Because she was not ready to let go of her mother.

Some nights, while she worked on her laptop and would get distracted by her mother's grunts and groans, she'd question that, wondering if, when her mother's time came, she'd be able to let go, knowing that her mother's pain had eased and she'd never hurt again. Then Carly would put the thoughts from her head, because she didn't want to think about when that horrible day arrived and how she'd deal with the loss.

She wasn't sure she could deal with losing her mother.

As they reached the entrance of the restaurant, he asked, "Do you do anything for fun, Carly?"

"Of course." But she didn't look at him.

"Name something."

"Sitting with my mother."

"That doesn't count."

"It should. There's no one else I'd rather spend time with."

"Outside your house," he redirected his question, "do you do anything for fun?"

"Joyce has already told you that I don't go anywhere, so that isn't a fair question."

"I like Joyce. She seems like a great lady."

"She is. I don't know what I'd do without her," Carly admitted as he opened the restaurant door for her. "She is a life-saver."

"My guess is that you'd manage," he said, smiling as she hesitated outside the restaurant entrance. "You seem the type to make things work no matter how much stress you endure in the process."

Which was one of the biggest compliments Stone could have given to her. She wanted to be independent, to handle things herself. It was what her mother had done, while healthy and capable, and it was what Carly strived for.

"Thank you," she told him and meant it as they entered the restaurant. Carly's stomach twisted at what she knew was likely to come. Or maybe she'd get lucky and all the people who'd known her would have moved on, just as she had. After all, she'd not been inside the restaurant for five years. "If I've come across as whiny—" she glanced around the restaurant and took in the bluesy atmosphere and smells that instantly filled her with nostalgia "—that wasn't my intention."

"You're not whiny. Far from it. I just stated my observation." He leaned forward and told the hostess, "Two."

Carly didn't recognize the young girl, nor had she seen a single person she recognized. She relaxed a little. A lot changed in five years. Not Julio's décor or atmosphere, though.

Same wooden tables with their battery lit candles. Same high-back chairs that were only semi-comfortable. Same rust-colored seats in the booths that lined one wall. Same jazzy blues playing softly in the background. She breathed in a deep breath. Same yummy garlic and tomato sauce smell.

Her stomach growled. She covered her belly with her hand and turned to see if the growl had been so thunderous that Stone had heard.

If so, he didn't point it out, just smiled and said, "I've been watching you for a month."

"That's creepy," she scolded. All the while her insides danced with a nervousness that had nothing to do with being creeped out and everything to do with the fact she was the object of this gorgeous man's attention.

"Not that I haven't told myself the same thing since overhearing your conversation with Rosalyn, but there's a comment that will deflate a man's ego in a hurry."

"I'd say your ego is just fine."

"Possibly not after the beating you've given it over the past two days."

"I enjoy talking with you at the hospital but we can't have a relationship outside the hospital," she pointed out. "I'm sorry if I let you think that was a possibility."

He studied her. "Because of your situation?"

She nodded. "Yes."

Holding a couple of menus, the hostess motioned for them to follow her. She seated them at one of the booths. Carly had always liked the booths and thought they were cozy and perfect for a date. Not that this was a date. Or maybe it was. She wasn't really sure.

When they were settled into their seats and the hostess had moved on, Stone asked, "Isn't the fair thing to give me the facts and let me decide for myself?"

He made a good point. One she couldn't think of a single argument against.

"I suppose." She stared at her menu.

"So why didn't you?"

Good question.

"I don't know." She stared at the menu harder, marveling that it was the same as when she'd worked there, other than an increase in prices.

"Not good enough."

Not glancing up, she shrugged. "It's the only answer I have."

"Dig deeper, Carly. Why didn't you let me make the choice for myself?"

He studied her so closely that she didn't have to look to feel the intensity.

"We all have baggage, Carly," he assured her. "Just different-sized suitcases."

Carly bit the inside of her cheek. He wasn't going to let this drop, which meant she really did have to dig deeper, and when she dug, she didn't like what she saw.

Lowering her menu, she met his gaze. "I was afraid to give you that option and set myself up for disappointment," she said, watching to see how he reacted to her admission.

"How would I disappoint you?"

Good grief, the man pushed. Why wasn't their waitress interrupting to get their drink orders?

"My life is full. Despite that I am with you now, this isn't typical. Nor can it be. I rush home from work and am there until I go back to work. I don't have time for dating or becoming involved with someone. I just don't," she emphasized the words, "and won't."

Then the waitress joined them, chatting away about what a lovely evening it was and could she tempt them with some fresh bread, which of course she could. She took their drink orders, then disappeared again.

"Maybe we can be friends."

Stone's words surprised Carly. "Friends?"

He reached across the table and took her hand. "Let's be friends. I get the impression you could use one."

His hand was warm around hers, but not warm enough to explain the fire moving through her body.

Fire that wasn't friendly.

Not by a long shot.

A flashback of him talking with Mrs. Kim, of how comforting his voice had been, how the woman's expression had eased, how they'd both ended up laughing, struck Carly.

Maybe Stone was right.

Maybe she did need a friend.

She'd had friends during college, but she'd put everything on hold to take care of her mother and work. Slowly, one by one, friends had faded away. Now, Carly had her co-workers, Joyce, and her mother.

"You want to be my friend?" The possibility didn't seem feasible. Why would he want to be her friend? Especially when she had little to offer a friendship?

"Let's be clear," he clarified, clasping her hand more firmly. "I want to be your lover."

Oh, God, had he really just said he wanted to be her lover?

"But I'll take being your friend if that's what you're willing to give."

CHAPTER FIVE

CARLY GULPED. HER LOVER. She hadn't been kissed in years, hadn't been touched in years.

Until meeting Stone she hadn't realized just how much she'd missed having someone touch her, want her.

Crazy. That was how Stone made her feel. Absolutely crazy.

"I'm not a very good friend," she admitted. She probably hadn't been a very good lover, either, but he didn't need to know that.

The waitress set their drinks on the table, then a basket of fresh bread.

When she was gone, he asked, "How so?"

"Friends require spending time together. I don't have time. As tempting as the idea of having someone in my life is, it simply won't work. To even try means robbing time from somewhere where I don't have time to spare. No matter how we sugar-coat the facts, they are still the facts. Tonight is an aberration that can't happen again."

He squeezed her hand. "No more serious talk. If tonight is an aberration, then let's make the most of it. What would you like for dinner?"

Glancing at the menu, her gaze landed on her favorite. Her mouth watered just at seeing the description. "The parmesan-crusted chicken is amazing."

His gaze lifted from the menu. "After your recommendation, I've come here a time or two, but haven't tried that yet."

"You should," she encouraged, hoping the amazingness of the dish hadn't been one of the things to change over the past five years, too. "Or you can get something different and I'll share my chicken."

Stone's smile set the butterflies back into motion in her belly.

"Deal."

Satisfied from the delicious meal, Stone stared across the table at the woman who fascinated him more and more. "So did your dad leave before or after you were born?"

Not immediately answering, she frowned. "I thought we weren't having any more serious conversation."

"We're not. At least not along the lines of our earlier conversation," he clarified, not wanting the relaxed atmosphere between them to dissipate. "Feel free to say pass on anything you don't want to answer."

He watched the play of emotions flash across her face and expected to hear, "Pass." Instead, she took a sip of her water, then gave a real answer.

"My dad wasn't ever in the picture," she began. "How did you know?"

"The lack of photos of him in the living room. There were lots of you, some of you and who I assume is your mother, and one of you with your mother and an older couple. Grandparents?"

She nodded. "He and my mother were never married. They lived together for a short while, before she moved back in with my grandparents, the house where we still live, actually. He was a construction worker and only stayed in an area long enough to finish the job. Then he would move to the next place, which is exactly what he did. I'm not sure if he offered to take my mother, but she stayed in Memphis. A month or so after he'd left, she discovered she was pregnant, and let him know. He told her he was sorry, sent money for an abortion. As far as I know, he has no clue that was never an option for her."

Amazed that Carly had revealed so much when he generally had to push for the tiniest tidbit of personal information, Stone reached for her hand, again. Raw emotions tossed his stomach's contents like a tumultuous sea at the feel of her small hand tucked beneath his.

"I'm glad that was never an option."

Carly smiled. A real smile and one that made Stone's chest tighten.

"The feeling is mutual."

Her smile made Stone long for a lot of things, things he might not ever have with Carly. His gut instinct told him to be patient and she would come around.

Exactly what all he wanted, he wasn't sure. He didn't see himself going down the marriage path again. But he would like a relationship with Carly for however long their attraction lasted. Besides, when Carly did start dating, she needed to experience life, freedom, rather than settle into a new commitment such as marriage or motherhood.

She'd clearly missed out on so much life had to offer.

During their friendship, he'd like to show her, give her, some of those missed-out-on things.

"So now that you know all about me, tell me about you," she turned the tables.

Turnabout was fair play. Not that Stone had much to hide, but, as he'd told her, every person came with baggage.

His was of the "ex-wife who'd walked out on their marriage" variety.

But he wasn't going there. Not tonight.

"Middle child of a middle-class family who live in the middle of nowhere."

"That's a lot of middles."

He nodded. "My dad's a dentist." He smiled, flashing perfectly straight white teeth. "My mom worked at the post office for twenty years, then decided she wanted to be a stay-home mom to my baby sister, who was ten at the time and not interested in having Mom around all the time."

"Ten? How old is your sister now?"

"Twenty. My oldest sister is thirty-five."

Carly's eyes widened. "Fifteen years? That's a big age gap. And, you're in the middle?"

He nodded. "I've not mentally delved into how Jenny came into existence. What kid wants to think about his parents' sex life? But I got the impression she was a surprise. Have you ever thought about tracking down your birth father?"

Carly shook her head. "Not once." At his look, she shrugged. "That may sound weird, but my mother was a very good mother. My grandparents, the best. I was a happy, content child. I never felt the need for anything more than what I had, because I had all the things that count. Plus, my biological father had his shot to be involved in my life and sent a strong message when my mother told him about me."

Stone flinched on the inside. Yeah, they all had baggage. Truer words had never been spoken.

"What?" she asked, obviously seeing more on his face than he'd meant her to see.

"You're an amazing person," he said, honestly.

Brow arched, she asked, "Because I had a good childhood?"

"That you are content with what you had," he clarified. "What you have. A lot of people would be bemoaning all they didn't have, that they were saddled with an ailing parent at such a young age. You seem to embrace all life throws at you."

"Ha. Embrace is not the right verb. I have my moments of boohooing and major pity-parties, especially when Mom is having a bad day. Don't think I don't or that there aren't times that I question why."

"You wouldn't be human if you didn't." Stone laced their fingers. "I'm glad you have me to help you now."

He would help her. He might not have been able to help Stephanie, but he could help lighten Carly's load, to add brightness to her life.

Carly winced. She didn't want to lean on anyone, didn't want to depend on someone to be there and them not be, and it to topple her world.

She was doing just fine on her own. Maybe that was partially why she'd kept the world shut out.

To depend on someone meant risking being let down, meant risking a weak link in the wall. She couldn't do that. Not when it came to her mother.

She had to make sure everything that could be done was being done. That she was doing her best to take care of her mother.

Carly didn't elaborate on any of that. She just ignored Stone's comment and changed the subject. "I would like to really bring Joyce dessert, if that's okay?"

"We can order one of every dessert on the menu if that's what you'd like to do."

Carly smiled as she imagined Joyce's delight at the silly gesture. "Really?"

He picked up the dessert menu. "There's four options, so we should bring her one of each. That way we're sure to get something she'll like. After all, it's thanks to her that I didn't have to eat alone."

Carly pinched every penny. Part of her cringed at the idea of wasted money, but the thought of Joyce's smile, of being a part of something that would bring happiness to her face, tempted way more than logic weighed in.

"I'd like to do that," she agreed, not bothering to point out that if Stone didn't want to eat alone, he'd never have to. Innumerous women would line up to keep him company. "I can pay half."

She'd have to cut corners elsewhere, but doing something sweet for Joyce would be worth it.

His brow arched. "Do you think I'd let you pay when I'm the one who offered to bring dessert?"

"You didn't offer to bring four desserts. I don't mind helping cover the cost."

"I'd mind if you did. Let me do this, Carly. It's not much and I want to." He waggled his brows. "We'll call the extra three desserts an investment."

Suspicion rallied in her belly. "An investment?"

"I want Joyce to like me."

Taking air into her tight chest hurt. "Because?"

"You and I are going to be friends. I can't have the person closest to you not liking me or she might not want me around."

Her head spun a little. "You plan to be around?"

His gaze didn't leave hers. "You said it yourself. Friends spend time together. I don't expect our friendship to be otherwise."

"I can't ask Joyce to stay late so I can spend time with you. Please don't think that's what tonight is leading to."

She sure couldn't afford to hire Joyce for extra hours. Doing so just wasn't in the budget. Not even if Carly forwent sleep and worked round the clock.

"Joyce doesn't have to stay late."

Carly stared, trying to figure out his game. "Then how?"

"Where there's a will there's a way." He didn't look concerned, just smiled that casual grin of his and motioned to their waitress so they could order four desserts to go.

Stone pulled into Carly's gravel drive and turned off the engine. She sat in the passenger seat, fiddling with her seat belt.

"Thank you for tonight."

"Even though I had to practically coerce you into going?" he teased, turning toward her.

"Hopefully you understand my reasons."

He considered her comment, then, "Partially."

"Well, it was a lovely evening, and I appreciate the opportunity to feel…somewhat normal, outside of work. Thank you."

Stone wondered what she had been going to say and searched her face, trying to see deep inside her mind, to know everything she was thinking, feeling.

"Any time, Carly. Any time."

She smiled, but it quickly disappeared.

"Shall I go in with you to give Joyce her desserts?"

She flinched. "You bought the desserts. Sending you away doesn't seem quite fair."

He'd hoped Carly would realize they could be friends, could make this work. Obviously, she wasn't on the same page. Not yet.

His gaze not wavering from hers, knowing what her answer was going to be, he asked, "But you'd rather I not come in?"

Carly took a deep breath. Insurance claims. Her mother. Bills. Answering the questions Joyce was sure to have. Berating herself for going to dinner with Stone. She had a long, long night ahead of her.

"As I said, tonight has been lovely." It truly had. A night she wasn't likely to forget any time soon and would replay over and over in her mind. A night where she felt like a semi-normal twenty-seven-year-old female. "If it's all the same, I'd like to say goodnight out here."

"It's not all the same, but I realize you worked a twelve-hour shift today and have to be exhausted."

He had no idea.

"So when I say goodnight, do you mean as in verbally saying goodnight or can I kiss you?"

Carly's heartbeat jumped into overdrive and she gripped the seat belt tighter to keep her hand from shaking. "How am I supposed to answer that without making things awkward between us?"

He considered her question a moment, then asked, "So I should have just leaned over and kissed you?"

His having done so would have been straight from a fantasy, but also a complication neither of them needed.

"Do friends kiss each other goodnight?"

"Good point." He stuck out his hand. "Goodnight, Carly. Thank you for going to dinner."

Carly's gaze dropped to his hand. He meant for her to shake it? Fighting confusion, she glanced back up.

He was going to shake her hand, not kiss her goodnight. Okay. Made sense. Hadn't she been preaching they couldn't have a romantic relationship all evening?

She put her hand in his and shook it in the strangest handshake. His grip was firm and gentle at the same time.

Calming and disturbing.

Warm and hot.

Right, yet all wrong.

"Are you working tomorrow?" he asked, still gripping her hand in a continuation of the awkward handshake. Why was he hanging on? Why was she?

She shook her head. "Today was my last of three on."

Not that she wouldn't be working over the next three days she had off from the hospital. She'd pull twelve-plus-hour days for the insurance company.

"I'd like to see you tomorrow. Before you tell me you can't, let me assure you that you can. I'd like to come by here after I finish at the hospital."

She bit the inside of her cheek, then ordered herself to stop. She was making a raw spot with how much she'd chewed at the area that day. Of all the ways of dealing with stress, she needed to find a nervous tic that was less self-destructive.

Stone wanted to come there tomorrow evening. Normally, she'd either be sitting with her mother or working, usually both.

"I'm not much of a cook if you're fishing for an invite to dinner." Cooking would mean going to the grocery store, which would mean getting Joyce to sit with her mother and dipping into her rainy-day fund. Which she'd already done once that month for her mother's new meds.

"I could pick up something for us. Just tell me what your mother eats."

"That isn't necessary. Besides, she chokes easily so is on a high nutrient, thick liquid diet."

His thumb brushed across the back of her hand in a slow caress. Were the lightning bolts of awareness shooting through her supposed to be friendly? They weren't. More like an assault on her nerve endings, setting them on high alert.

"Getting Mom to take in anything by mouth is a chore." Not that she and Joyce didn't do their best every single meal. Continuing to take in meals via normal methods was important mentally and emotionally—for her mother and for Carly. "She gets most of her nutrition through her feeding tube, unfortunately."

How ill her mother was seemed to finally click, and Stone's grip on her hand tightened. "I'm sorry, Carly."

The pity in his voice raised walls of annoyance. She didn't want his pity. She didn't need his pity.

Taking a deep breath, she made herself step back, made herself allow him to express his empathy without her going on the defensive. Hard to do because she'd had years of keeping her chin held high.

"It is what it is."

He sat quietly a moment, then asked, "It's okay if I bring you dinner?"

Carly's chest ached at the sincerity in his voice. He wanted her to say yes. He wanted to spend time with her.

She had so much work to do.

But if she had to sit up all night without sleeping, it would be worth it to spend more time with Stone.

"You realize I can't have a normal friendship with you? That you're wasting your time if you're hoping for something more?"

"What's normal, Carly?"

He made a good point. What was normal? Were there any easy, perfect relationships out there? When she'd dated back in her university days everything had seemed easy, but maybe that hadn't been a true reflection of life. Not that they were talking dating. They weren't. They were going to be friends.

Friends with Stone.

"I suppose it wouldn't do any good to offer to give you money to cover my portion?" she asked, conceding to his request against her better judgment.

"You suppose correctly." His smile was so bright it almost lit the car. His dad must be a fabulous dentist. "I'll see you tomorrow evening."

She pulled her hand free and opened the car door. Before getting out, she hesitated. "If you don't show, if you change your mind about our friendship, I'll understand."

He opened his door, came around, took the dessert bag from her and walked her to her front door. "If I don't show, call 911 because something major happened on my way here."

Staring into his green eyes, she nodded, but still didn't quite let herself believe.

"Goodnight, Carly. I will see you tomorrow."

With that, he bent, kissed her cheek, and whistled as he walked back to his car.

Carly stared after him long after he'd driven away in his fancy SUV, wondering what in the world she'd gotten herself into and why she hadn't stopped it.

Why she'd ever let it get started to begin with.

She couldn't blame Stone.

She'd been the one to know the crazy details of her life. Yet she had spent time with him, had a few flirty conversations, given him her address.

Wanting him as her friend hadn't motivated any of those things.

Her suddenly come-to-life raging hormones that had been dead for five years had taken over her brain and body.

CHAPTER SIX

THE NEXT MORNING, Mrs. Kim's wound wasn't any better.

Stone ordered a new culture, added an additional intravenous antibiotic and talked with her family about keeping her at the hospital longer.

He spent most of the day doing routine procedures, but did have a more intensive mastectomy scheduled for the afternoon.

Every time he was in between high concentration, his mind drifted to Carly.

She had a lot more going on than met the eye. He wanted to lighten her load. He just wasn't sure how to go about it without offending or pushing her away. She was as touchy as the most delicate flower. If he pushed too hard, she'd wither and refuse to let him in.

"So how did your conversation the other day go with my favorite nurse?"

Stone glanced up from the hospital computer at Rosalyn and he grinned. "She's my favorite nurse, too, you know?"

"Oh, I know." Rosalyn laughed. "Not going to tell me details, huh? Neither would she and I've asked her more than once."

"Some things are better kept private."

Rosalyn's eyes brightened. "Oh?"

"Not those things," Stone quickly assured her. "We've decided to be friends."

Rosalyn frowned. "I'm not sure if that makes you the world's dumbest man or her the dumbest woman. Or both."

He chuckled. "Nothing wrong with being friends."

"Except for when you both want more."

"What makes you think Carly wants more?" Yes, his question was self-serving because he wanted Rosalyn to confirm what he knew deep in his gut. Carly was interested in him, but didn't think she had time. He'd just have to make himself so useful that she'd realize his being around made her life better, easier.

Rosalyn tsked teasingly at him. "You're showing your 'more than just want to be friends' interest," she accused.

"Which you already knew since you were the one informing Carly I had the hots for her."

She gave him a "so what?" look. "I didn't hear you denying it."

"Nor will you."

A pleased smile spread across her face. "Carly is a hard worker, always positive, never complains about anything, nor says anything negative about anyone. But sometimes, when she thinks no one is looking, I see the truth on her face and get the impression she has a hard life."

Rosalyn wasn't wrong, but it wasn't Stone's place to fill in the gaps.

"That said, in the five or so years I've known her, not once has she been distracted from her job."

"Now she is?"

"Oh, she's still an excellent nurse, one of the best, but for the past month she gets dreamy-eyed."

It was Stone's turn to smile. "Wonder what happened a month ago to put that look in her eyes?"

"I wonder." Rosalyn's face took on a motherly expression. "All I have to say is you'd better not hurt that girl 'cause I think someone must have done a real number on her in the past."

Carly hadn't mentioned someone in her past, but certainly there could have been. Stone didn't like the idea of a man in Carly's past, especially not one who'd hurt her. Maybe her mother had always been ill and the effects of that was what Rosalyn had picked up on.

"I've no intention to hurt Carly." Quite the opposite. He wanted to make her life better. To take away the darkness and fill her world with sunshine. As much sunshine as he could beam her way when she was dealing with such a tragic situation. She needed his help whether she knew it or not.

Rosalyn's almost black eyes narrowed in warning. "Some pain isn't from intentional infliction."

"Point taken." Not that he didn't already know firsthand. He'd never meant to hurt Stephanie, but had. Or was it the opposite? If only she'd let him help her, how different would their situation have been?

"Just you be good to that girl or stay away from her is all I'm saying."

"Yes, ma'am," he assured Rosalyn. "Now tell me about my new surgical consult in Room 210. An abdominal pain?"

Carly stood from the chair next to her mother's hospital bed and stretched her aching muscles. She'd worked late into the night, set her alarm and gotten up early to work several hours, then fed and bathed her mother, got her out of bed and into her wheelchair, and taken her out for a stroll down their bumpy sidewalk.

She hated her mother being cooped up in the house all the time, but, even with the mechanical lift, getting her in and out of her bed was becoming more difficult.

Eventually, Carly wasn't going to be able to manage and would have to have more help. Either that or put her mother in a nursing home.

She hoped it never came to that.

Sometimes that was the only option. However, she was a nurse. She knew how to provide her mother's care. Though she just might reach the point where she didn't have the resources to do so in the manner best for her mother.

If that day came, Carly would have hard decisions to face. Decisions she didn't know how she'd make.

She glanced at where her mother slept. She now slept more than she was awake. Which could be a side effect of her medications as much as a symptom of her disease. Either way, Carly appreciated the moments when her mother was awake, lucid, and not in horrid pain.

Like earlier that day when they'd been on their stroll.

Although her mother had called her Margaret, she'd enjoyed the fresh air, had commented on the squirrels they'd seen, had told Carly they needed to hire someone to fix the loose boards on the front porch railing.

Audrey hadn't used the front door in years as her handicap ramp was located on the back of the house, but obviously she still paid attention. The house needed new paint, gutters, landscaping, and a new roof. Just for starters. Every time it rained, Carly feared that that would be the time the iffy-looking roof finally gave in to the weather.

She glanced around her mother's bedroom at the dingy paint, at the photos of the two of them that hung on the wall, at the dresser that held the same perfume bottles from half a decade ago.

"Wh-what a-are y-you th-thinking?"

Her mother's words were low, soft, garbled, but Carly's ears were trained to understand her speech.

"That I should spruce this place up."

Her mother shook her head. "Don't th-think y-you n-need to do th-that on m-my a-account."

"I was thinking more for my account. This place looks exactly as it did when I was in elementary school."

"I-I'm t-too old for ch-change."

Interesting. Was her mother saying that because she truly liked being surrounded by the way things had been or because change confused her?

"You're not that old," Carly countered, smiling at her mother and wondering if she knew she was Carly or if she thought she was Margaret.

Her mother chuckled, making Carly's heart swell.

"I-If you're a-as o-old as y-you feel th-then I-I'm a-ancient."

Carly bent and kissed her mother's cheek. "It's the medicine making you feel that way."

"I-It's my b-body ma-making me f-feel that w-way," her mother corrected. "H-Help me s-sit up."

Carly did so, raising the head of the hospital bed, then repositioning her mother's pillows. She fed her mother as much as she could get her to eat by mouth, which was only a few bites, then fed her the specially formulated liquid meal via her feeding tube.

"Is there anything I can get you? Anything you want?" Carly asked her mother that question every day. Her mother almost always gave the same answer, saying she was fine and didn't need anything.

That day she had Carly's jaw dropping.

"A g-grandk-kid."

Carly stared in disbelief. She'd never heard her mother say such a thing. Or even hint at such a desire.

Not knowing how to respond, Carly gave a shaky laugh. "This one may take a little time as I'll need to find a sperm donor. Plus, there's that whole incubation-for-nine-months thing."

Her mother shook her head. "D-don't do it l-like I—I did. F-find a-a man wh-who'll st-stick around."

"Okay, Mom."

"Th-that d-doctor f-friend, m-maybe."

"Stone? Er… Dr. Parker, I mean?" Carly gulped and didn't meet her mother's still-shrewd gaze. She really shouldn't have gone on about Stone the other night. No wonder her mother was getting ideas. Especially if Joyce had mentioned Carly going to dinner with him. Carly hadn't asked her not to, but had hoped she wouldn't. "I…we're just friends, Momma, but…he is a nice man and a wonderful surgeon. And kind. He's very kind. I like that about him."

There she went on about Stone again. She really needed to stop doing that.

When Carly looked up, her gaze collided with her mother's. But her mother just smiled and closed her eyes. Within seconds her breathing had evened out, indicating she'd drifted into sleep again, leaving Carly to consider their conversation.

She couldn't recall her mother having mentioned grandchildren. Not even once. At least not in a manner other than a passing thought that some day Carly would make her a grandma. That had been years ago. Back when they'd both thought Carly's life would be very different.

When they'd thought Audrey's life would be very different.

If only some pharmaceutical company could come up with a cure. Carly would give most anything to see the strong, vibrant woman her mother had once been.

Maybe some day a cure would exist, but, realistically, Carly knew any such treatment wouldn't be in time to save her mother.

Tears pricked her eyes. *Stop it,* she scolded herself. She had no time for self-pity. Especially when the woman lying in the hospital bed never showed any. No complaints, just acceptance that life was what it was.

Was there a connection to Carly having mentioned Stone and the sudden request for grandchildren? If so, her mother would be sadly disappointed. Last night with Stone had been wonderful but Carly didn't expect anything more. Probably, truth be told, the best thing that could happen would be if Stone realized how problematic her life was and forgot she existed.

Certainly, that would be best for him.

After running through a few stretches to protect her spine, Carly sat back down in the chair next to her sleeping mother's hospital bed. She glanced at her watch, wondered where the morning had gone, then dove back into the insurance claims.

Tedious work, but someone had to do it. Since she could work from home and had some control over when she worked, Carly was the woman for the job.

When a knock sounded at her door, Carly jumped, almost dropping her laptop.

She hadn't realized just how much time had passed.

Which was to her advantage because if she had, she'd have been distracted with wondering if Stone would show or not. Would have been anxiously listening for sounds of his arrival and wondering if she was being foolish.

He'd come.

Well, it was possible someone else was at her door, but it was unlikely. She didn't have company. Just Joyce, herself, and her mother were ever at the house.

But Stone had come. He'd said he would and he had. Her crazy life hadn't scared him away.

Standing up, stretching once again because of how long she'd been curled up in the chair and the fact her legs were numb, she then headed to her front door.

Her heart pounded and she felt breathy.

As if she were running a race rather than casually walking through her house.

She stepped up to the front door. Through the screen window, she could see Stone.

A very gorgeous Stone.

The man was really too good-looking to be real. Those eyes belonged to some paranormal hero in a supernatural television show.

And his mouth. A lush, kissable mouth that curved

into such an amazing smile. Must come from being a dentist's son.

Friends. They were just going to be friends. Nothing more.

This was okay. Sort of.

"I see there's no need for me to call 911," she teased, opening the door. Then, taking in the number of bags he held, she frowned. "Good grief, how much do you expect me to eat?"

He grinned. "I decided to cook dinner, rather than bring take-out."

She blinked. He was going to cook? "Which doesn't answer my question. Do I look like I have that big of an appetite?"

He laughed. "You're perfect just as you are, so whatever your appetite, it suits you."

Perfect. Her. Ha.

"If I didn't know better I'd think you were Irish and blessed with the Blarney Stone."

His grin was breathtaking. "I wasn't sure what you had in your kitchen," he admitted, "so I bought everything I'd need."

What if she didn't want him in her barren kitchen?

What if take-out felt less personal than him cooking?

What if she was so glad to see him, that he'd shown up, that she wanted to throw her arms around him and hug him? As a friend, of course.

"I don't know what to say."

"I'd say 'thank you', but you should probably wait until after you've eaten." He waggled his brows. "My mother and sisters are good cooks. I'm a decent cook, but make no promises on edibility."

"What are we having?"

"Homemade spaghetti and meatballs, garlic bread, and I brought a couple of different wines to choose from."

She rarely drank alcohol as it tended to make her sleepy, but she nodded. "Sounds good."

"Point me to your kitchen and I'll go back to get the rest of the bags."

She blinked. "There's more?"

"I told you, I wasn't sure if you'd have all the ingredients. Now, give me directions on which way to go."

She pointed down the hallway. "The house is only two bedrooms, so I doubt you'd get lost, but the kitchen is the first door to the right."

"Perfect."

She followed him into the kitchen, watched a little in awe as he set down the bags on her once bright yellow Formica countertops. "Can I help?"

"I'm counting on it."

That was good because she couldn't imagine just watching him work while she did nothing. How awkward would that be?

"Just tell me what to do."

"Come here."

Not knowing what he planned, she came close to where he stood, gasping when he wrapped his arms around her waist and pulled her to him.

With the embrace, she halfway expected him to kiss her, but instead he just grinned down at her.

"Did you think about me today?"

A zillion times. Plus, I'm pretty sure my mother wants us to give her grandchildren and she's not even met you. "Was I supposed to?"

His thumbs tracing across her low back, he laughed. "You are such an ego-buster."

His fingers were magical because all kinds of things were happening inside her body. Would it be wrong if she closed her eyes and just pretended this was so much more?

"Sorry." She was smiling back at him. How could she

not? "I didn't know thinking of you was a condition of our friendship."

"Thinking about each other is definitely a condition of our friendship."

"I'll keep that in mind tomorrow and make sure I think of you at least once."

He chuckled. "You do that."

His hands rested low on her back. His body pressed hard against her belly. Carly's knees wobbled. Had to have because she leaned into him.

She looked at him, parted her lips, waited in anticipation of whatever he had in mind when he'd pulled her close.

He stared into her eyes, then grinned as if nothing out of the ordinary was happening. Maybe it wasn't.

"I'm going to grab the other bags. You mind unpacking these?"

"I…" She glanced at the bags he'd put on her countertop. "Sure."

With that he was out of the room. When she heard the front screen door open and close, she sighed.

Okay, what had that been? A friendly hug?

Stone paused on Carly's front porch and took a deep breath. What had he been thinking to pull her into his arms?

When he'd gotten her there, he hadn't wanted to let go, had had to force himself to step away.

Because when he'd looked into her eyes, he'd seen awareness. Physical awareness. And curiosity. She'd wondered if he was going to kiss her and the idea had intrigued her.

Which had done crazy, stupid things to his insides.

Like make all his blood rush south.

He couldn't kiss Carly. No matter the look she'd given. She needed their friendship and he'd give it to her.

A few loose boards on the porch caught his eye and he mentally tallied what he'd need to fix them.

He'd get the rest of the groceries, cook Carly dinner, and make a mental list of things he could help with around her house.

Carly took in the bags on her counter. More bags than she'd bought at one time in years. Maybe ever.

Why was Stone doing this?

Catching the tender flesh of her inner cheek between her teeth, Carly forced herself to stop over-thinking and began pulling fresh vegetables from the grocery bags.

When Stone had said he intended to cook her home-made, he'd meant homemade right down to the sauce apparently. Wow.

He made two additional trips out to his SUV and by the time he'd finished, her countertops were full.

"There's no way we can eat all this."

"We'll eat more than you think."

She glanced at all the food they'd unpacked. "I don't eat this much in a month."

"Which explains why you're so thin. You need to eat more."

He thought she was too thin? She glanced down. She wore loose black yoga pants and a baggy cotton gray T-shirt that was one of the most comfortable items she owned. Not as nice as his khaki trousers and expensive navy polo, but much more practical for how she'd spent her day.

"So much for your perfect comment earlier," she reminded, holding her hand up to stop him when he went to explain away his comment on her figure. "Doesn't matter. I've always been small framed. I take after my mom that way."

He leaned back against the countertop. "Will I meet her tonight?"

She had already wondered that, had wondered how she would explain Stone's presence when her mother woke.

"I'm sure you will."

"Good. It's obvious how much you adore and admire her. I can't wait to meet her."

Protectiveness hitting her, Carly hesitated. "She's been ill a long time. She's not the woman she used to be. Not on the outside."

"Mentally, she's good?"

"Sometimes," Carly told him, deciding to be as open as possible. Why not? He'd soon see for himself how ill her mother was. "Parkinson's disease is her main issue, but she has some vascular dementia as well, possibly from mini-strokes a couple of years ago or maybe from medications or the Parkinson's itself. The doctors aren't sure. More often than not, she thinks I'm her mother, Margaret. Sometimes, she's with me, knows me, and is my mother."

Stone winced. "I truly am sorry you have to deal with this."

There went the pity.

"Don't be," she told him, without looking directly at him because she didn't want to see that in his eyes. "Some people don't have mothers. Feel sorry for them. I'm lucky because I have mine."

There were a few moments of silence, then he said, "You make me feel as if I should call my mom and tell her how much I love and appreciate her."

Carly's eyes prickled with a little moisture at his sentiment. "You should."

"I'll do that."

But he must have meant later, because, rather than whip out his phone, he began washing off vegetables and whistling a tune she recognized but couldn't put her finger on.

"How can I help?"

"Find a cutting board and a sharp knife."

Carly found an old wooden cutting board and the sharpest knife she owned. Stone didn't look overly impressed. To his credit, he didn't say a word, just took the proffered items.

"I'm going to need a skillet for the sauce and a pan to cook the pasta."

"Right." Carly began digging in the cabinet, found a pan and an old cast-iron skillet that had been her grandmother's.

"That'll do," Stone said, eyeing her offerings. "Nice skillet."

If he said so. She could only recall a handful of times of having used the heavy thing. Memories of her mother using it to cook breakfast and the scent of bacon filling the entire house flashed through Carly's mind. The memory made her smile. She'd had a great childhood and was lucky.

"I take it you really do cook?"

He shot her a mischievous look. "Not often, because what's the fun in cooking for one?"

Not a lot. Which was why she lived on soups a lot. She could make a crockpot of soup and eat on it for a week. It was fairly healthy, easy to make, and inexpensive.

"We both know that if you eat alone it's by choice." She watched as he spread out items on the cutting board.

"The same could be said for you."

"I have a different set of circumstances," she reminded him. "I can't be out. I'm needed at home. I want to be at home," she corrected.

"I've said it before, but where there's a will there's a way." He held up an onion. "Do you have a food processor?"

She held up her hands. "Just these, and a blender if that would work?"

"I take it you don't cook a lot."

"Not much."

"Since I know you usually bring your lunch to work that surprises me."

"Maybe I'm just not a fan of hospital cafeteria food."

"Our hospital's food is pretty good."

Carly couldn't argue. On the few occasions she'd eaten in the cafeteria, it had been well prepared.

Carly's watch alarm went off. "I'm going to bail on you for a few minutes. Maybe longer."

His brow rose.

"I keep Mom on a schedule—that way she gets proper nutrition. I wasn't thinking about the time when I offered to help. Not that I'd likely have been much help, anyway."

"Not a problem. Do what you need to do."

Before leaving the kitchen, Carly mixed the high calorie and nutrient food packet prescribed for her mother's feeding tube. She took out a small container of fresh fruit and blended it to a thick liquid consistency.

"Sorry, I'm bailing," she apologized again.

"It's probably better if you aren't here to watch." He winked. "You might be one of those who flip out if the cook licks the spoon."

"You don't?" she said in a faux-horrified voice.

"Leave now so you can keep thinking that."

Carly laughed, grabbed up the tray she'd put her mother's meal and supplies on, and left the kitchen.

When she went into her mother's room, Audrey was awake, which instantly struck Carly with guilt.

"Sorry, Mom, I didn't realize you were awake or I'd have been in here."

Her mother didn't say anything, just eyed the tray. "N-not h-hungry."

Which was the same thing she said at every meal. If not for the feeding tube, her mother would have withered into nothingness long ago.

"Try to eat a little." Which was the same thing Carly said at every meal. "We have to keep your strength up."

Sighing, looking exhausted, her mother nodded. Although her tremor made feeding herself almost impossible, Carly always let her mother attempt to before taking over the process. More food ended up on her mother than in her, but she wanted some normalcy to her mother's life.

Not that her daughter putting an adult-sized bib on her was normal.

Carly secured the bib, protecting her mother's gown, and her bed coverings. "Do you want me to get you out of bed to eat or do you want to eat here?"

She always gave her mother the choice. Getting out of the bed tired her out tremendously, but on the occasions her mother wanted to get out of the bed for her meal, she always seemed to eat a little more.

Plus, Carly wanted her out of the bed as much as possible. The more her mother felt like getting up, the better.

Today wasn't going to be one of those occasions, though, as her mother shook her head. "T-Too t-tired."

Which was how her mother felt most of the time. Still, between Joyce and Carly, they always got her out of bed at least once and put her in her wheelchair. On pretty days, they'd go for a short walk. Others they'd just push her into the living room to watch television or sit to talk to Carly or her caregiver.

Removing the food for the feeding tube, Carly put the bed tray over her mother's lap. Then, she put the small dish of thickened fruit on the tray, along with a special spoon that was supposed to help prevent food from spilling due to her tremor. It helped a little.

Her mother stared at the food for a few moments, then, seeming to will herself to do so, she slowly and shakily scooped up a bite and made it to her mouth.

Not on the first try, but she did get some of the puréed food there.

Carly wiped the dribble of food away from her mother's chin. "That was great, Mom. I know it's a lot of effort, but it makes me happy that you're eating."

Her mother didn't say anything, just slowly proceeded to take a few more bites. Carly cleaned spills in between each bite because she couldn't stand to see her mother, who'd always prided herself on her neat appearance, with globs of food stuck to her face.

After five or six bites, her mother dropped the spoon onto the tray.

"Full already?" Carly kept her smile in place. "Can't you try just one more?"

Her nursing experience had taught her that the more 'normal' things her mother did, the better her prognosis.

Which was why she or Joyce brushed and styled her mother's hair daily, why they put lipstick on her, why they kept her in pretty nightgowns Carly had picked up at the local second-hand store.

Expression tired, her mother shook her head.

Wishing she could have gotten her to eat more, Carly flushed the tube, administered the meal, then flushed the tube again. Then, she sat, talking to her mother, mostly about the more interesting insurance claims. Carly didn't reveal any personal information, just whatever the incident was that had triggered the claim. Some of the more interesting ones would get a smile from her mother, but her mother rarely spoke during the chit-chat.

"Wh-what's th-that sm-smell?"

Yeah, Carly was smelling it, too. Wonderful, mouth-watering smells drifting their way from the kitchen.

She'd gotten so wrapped up in her mother she'd completely forgotten about Stone.

How could she have forgotten the hunk in her kitchen?

First biting the inside of her cheek, she met her mother's curious gaze and then shrugged as if her next words were no big deal.

"I...uh... I have a friend over for dinner."

CHAPTER SEVEN

DESPITE CARLY'S ATTEMPT at nonchalance, her mother wasn't buying it.

No wonder. Carly hadn't had company, not counting Joyce and a few home-health nurses, in years. Not since Tony.

Her mother's eyes widened.

"A man," she added, because she knew what her mother's next question was going to be. "But don't get any ideas because we're just friends."

The former fatigue on her mother's face lifted significantly. "H-help m-me in—in my wh-wheelchair."

Her mother wanted to get out of bed a second time that day? Carly's heart swelled with joy. And maybe a little anxiety. She knew why her mother wanted out of bed.

"Yes, ma'am."

Carly repositioned the hospital bed to where it would be easiest to use the lift. She positioned everything just so to make that transition as smooth as possible, then assisted her mother into the chair.

"Maybe you'll want to eat with us," Carly suggested, slipping soft, fuzzy house shoes onto her mother's socked feet. "Seeing how much food he brought, I'm sure there is going to be plenty."

"Wh-who is h-he?"

"A surgeon at the hospital. He moved here about a month

ago. I told you about him when we were talking the other night. Remember?" Carly kept her voice light, cheerful, but hopefully not overly so. After her mother's comment about a grandchild, she didn't want her pulling Stone into that equation. "He's a great guy. Everyone likes him."

Why was she defending Stone? If her mother didn't like him, what did it matter? He was a co-worker, someone who wanted to be her friend.

It did matter.

A lot.

She wanted her mother to like Stone.

Which was why Carly was nervous as she straightened her mother in the wheelchair, made sure her gown was nice and neat, finger-styled her mother's hair back into place, then pushed her to the living area.

Hearing her moving about, Stone called from the kitchen, "Dinner is almost done."

"Smells good," she responded, glancing at her mother. If she could, Audrey would be out of her chair and into the kitchen quick as a flash. "Stone," she called, taking her clammy hands off the wheelchair grips and wiping them across her yoga pants. "When you can, I'd like you to meet my mother."

"Let me take the bread out, turn the sauce down to simmer, then I'll be right there."

Wondering why she was so edgy at the prospect of her mother meeting him, Carly fought the urge to wring her hands. Instead, she wrapped her fingers around the wheelchair grips while she settled her mother into "her" spot in the living room. A prime open area where there was no furniture, just worn hardwood flooring.

Against a wall was a television that was as deep as it was wide, attesting to its age. A small loveseat-size sofa and a sturdy wooden rocking chair that had been Carly's grandmother's were also in the room. In the far corner was a small round dining table with three chairs. The fourth spot was reserved for her mother, although she rarely felt up to eating meals at the table. A wooden bench was pushed against a wall. Pictures of Carly graced the wall. Her first birthday. Her sweet sixteen. Her high-school graduation shot.

There were a few family photos taken at a local department store that featured Carly and her mother. And Carly's favorite, which was a photo of her grandparents, her mother, and Carly sitting in her mother's lap. Both of her grandparents had died from natural causes within a few years of the photo.

Other than getting rid of a recliner and sofa that had matched the loveseat to make a spot for her mother's wheelchair, the room hadn't changed in years.

What had Stone thought of her home?

Had he judged her the other night when he'd dropped off the box? If so, he'd still come back.

With groceries to cook a meal.

Did he feel sorry for her? Was that what his real interest was? She was his charity project?

If Stone didn't like her home, he could leave. If it wasn't up to his standards, he could leave. If he pitied her, well, he'd better keep it hidden or she'd boot him. She didn't need or want his, or anyone's, charity.

If her mother didn't like Stone, no big deal.

She'd say goodbye and life would go on. He was a co-worker. Possibly a friend. A fantasy all kinds of things.

She positioned her mother to where she could see the television and the hallway where Stone would appear.

"Y-you've n-not br-brought a m-man h-home s-since T-Tony," her mother pointed out, watching Carly too closely for comfort.

She'd not brought anyone, male or female, except Tony, home in years.

"Remember he's just a friend, Momma," Carly reminded her. Okay, so Carly was struggling with remembering that herself. Maybe she needed to convince herself that he felt sorry for her so she could use anger to push him away.

"A very good friend," Stone added as he walked into the room, bent, and held out his hand to Carly's mom.

Intentional movement was a major problem for her mother and that seemed to hit Stone after his hand was in the air a moment longer than it should have been. Rather than wait on Audrey to shakily respond, he lowered to a squatting position, placed his hand over hers, and looked Carly's mom straight in the eyes.

"It's very nice to meet you, Ms. Evans." His smile was enough to dazzle anyone. His dad should use him as an advertisement; make him wear buttons promoting his dental practice. "I've heard a lot about you from Carly."

Carly's mother's gaze cut to her. "Sh-she's not s-said m-much about y-you."

"That's because I'm new in town and she's still trying to figure me out." Stone's charm was on full blast. Plus, he was still squatting, holding her mother's hand.

"Wh-what's sh-she go-going to f-find?"

Stone chuckled, then his expression took on a more serious look. "I'd like to say all good, to assure you there was nothing that wasn't pure white in my past, but we all have skeletons in our closets."

Carly found his comment odd as he'd made that implication previously when speaking about baggage. She couldn't imagine Stone having many skeletons in his closet and if he did they were probably the plastic, non-scary Halloween version.

Her mother studied him a few moments from behind her glasses, her gaze shrewd and assessing. Then, in testament to how much his being there motivated her, she cradled his hand between her trembling ones.

Carly fought gasping. Movement was painful for her mother, was awkward and shaky and difficult. Yet, she patted Stone's hand between hers as if it were the most natural thing in the world.

Maybe it was.

Just like that, Stone captivated her mother.

"I've cooked spaghetti and meatballs, my grandmother's recipe. Can I tempt you to join us?"

To Carly's surprise, or maybe not surprise since Stone had cast a spell over her mother, Audrey said yes.

Without slurring.

That her mother had already eaten the few bites, had had her feeding-tube meal, and still wanted to taste Stone's cooking had Carly wanting to kiss him.

Okay, maybe she'd wanted to kiss him before that, but definitely she owed him for the spark of life he'd put into her mother's eyes.

Stone unlocked the wheelchair, pushed Audrey over to the small wooden dining table on the opposite side of the room, and situated her at the table.

"She chokes easily," Carly reminded him when Stone started dipping some food out. "She can only have thickened liquids to keep her from aspirating."

"One b-bite is-isn't go-going to h-hurt m-me," her mother insisted, sounding annoyed at Carly. "I-If i-it g-goes d-down wr-wrong, th-there's a d-doctor h-here."

There was that.

Carly was more worried about aspiration pneumonia than her mother choking, though. It wouldn't take much for her food to end up in her lungs rather than her stomach. Even with the puréed bites, it was a risk.

"Can I help you?" Carly's teeth sank into the tender area on the inside of her cheek. Maybe, just maybe, her mother would chew every bite well and her throat would work properly and prevent aspiration.

Her mother shook her head. "H-him."

Stone shot a look to Carly, one that asked permission.

Carly nodded.

To his credit and Carly's relief, Stone used his fork to mash up the spaghetti to a mushy consistency. When he was satisfied with it, he took a small amount on his fork, managing not to get any pieces of the crumbled hamburger meat, and offered it to Carly's mother.

Audrey closed her eyes. Pleasure on her face, she chewed slowly for a long time. Neither Carly nor Stone said anything, just watched her, ready to jump into action at the slightest difficulty.

When Audrey opened her eyes, she smiled. "A m-man wh-who c-can c-cook is h-hard to f-find."

Stone grinned. "Unfortunately, I only have a few meals in my repertoire. I'm a quick study, though."

"B-bet y-you are."

Stone fed her another small mushed-up bite.

Carly watched in fascination at how her mother responded to him. She only ate a handful of small bites, but, as she'd already eaten some of the fruit and had her feeding-tube meal, Carly was impressed.

Her mother hadn't taken in that much by mouth in a long, long time.

"I may have you over every meal," Carly mused.

"That can be arranged," he offered, eyes sparkling and a grin on his face.

Carly's mother's gaze went from Stone to Carly and back again.

Carly's cheeks heated.

She didn't want her mother to get ideas. If Stone wasn't careful her mother would be picking out names for grandkids before he left that evening.

Somehow, she didn't think that was what he'd had in mind when he'd said he wanted them to be friends.

Carly took a bite, redirecting her mind so she didn't blush. At the burst of deliciousness in her mouth, she glanced toward Stone in true appreciation.

"Dinner is excellent," she praised, trying not to let her

surprise show. Then again, she should have known the meal would be superb. No doubt, anything he did was. "Thank you."

This was the Carly who had caught Stone's attention at the hospital. A smiling one. A laughing one. Her mother sat with them, but said very little while he and Carly ate and talked.

He told tales about his family, recounting a few humorous tales of his two sisters that had both Evans women laughing.

"Yeah, Jenny is a troublemaker, for sure."

"No wonder with you as her mentor," Carly pointed out.

"I might have taught her a thing or two." He winked. "Either way, we're both very different from Paula. She's the serious one of the bunch."

"What does she do?"

"She's an infectious disease specialist in Atlanta. Works for the CDC."

"A doctor?" Carly asked, looking genuinely impressed.

"Yes. She's more into research than dealing with actual people."

"What's Jenny interested in?"

"Boys."

At Carly's raised brow, Stone continued.

"She's twenty, but isn't sure what she wants to do when she 'grows up'. Or if she wants to grow up."

"It must have been difficult to grow up in the shadow of you and your sister, constantly being compared to two overachievers."

"Paula is the overachiever, not me."

Carly's gaze narrowed. "Have you ever failed at anything you've set your mind out to do?"

"More often than I care to admit." That squeezing pain he always got when thinking of Stephanie shot across his chest. To redirect the conversation away from his biggest failure, he gestured to the table. "There's quite a bit left."

Carly looked at the large glass bowl he'd filled with spaghetti, at the basket he'd put garlic bread into.

"You want to take it home?" she offered. "I'm sure I can find some containers."

He shook his head. "I'll be in surgery most of the day tomorrow so I'll grab something at the hospital. If it won't go to waste, I'll leave it here."

"Something that tastes this good won't go to waste," she assured him. "Joyce is going to think she's in heaven when I share."

He flashed his dentist's kid smile.

"By the way, Joyce about fell over herself at her desserts." She smiled. "She had to taste them all here and made me take a bite of each, too."

He knew he liked Joyce. "Did she have a favorite?"

"The lava cake."

"Sounds good. We should have done dessert last night."

"No way." She shook her head. "I was much too full to have dessert."

"But you did try a bite of each?"

Carly's lips curved upward. "She insisted."

"Did you have a favorite?"

"The apple cobbler." Her face filled with remembered pleasure. "The ice cream had melted into a soup, but it was still fantastic."

"Wh-when w-was th-this?" her mother asked, her gaze going back and forth between them.

Carly's look of pleasure morphed into one of guilt.

"Stone followed me home last night after work so he could carry in a box." Carly's voice was overly bright. "You were asleep, but Joyce met him and stayed so we could go to dinner. Stone brought her back four different desserts from Julio's." Carly smiled. "Wasn't that nice of him?"

"J-Julio's wh-where you w-worked?"

Carly had worked at the restaurant where they'd gone? Why hadn't she said anything?

"Yes, but I didn't see anyone I knew." She cast a nervous glance toward Stone. "Everything looks the same except for the people working there."

Her mother nodded, then looked Stone dead in the eyes. Her eyes were a similar shade of honey brown as Carly's, only sharper, shrewder. "Wh-what are y-your in-intentions?"

Stone hesitated. He and Carly had agreed to be friends, nothing more. Yes, he wanted more, but the bright red glow to Carly's face warned that he needed to proceed with caution on how he answered.

"And that's why I don't normally bring men home," Carly cut in with a feigned teasing tone. "Mom, I told you, Stone and I are just friends."

"Good friends," Stone added, watching Carly's face for her reaction. He got one. Wide eyes and open mouth.

He also got one from Carly's mother. A smile and look of approval.

"Yes, we're becoming good friends since Stone moved here," Carly rushed out, waving off his comment. "Good friends don't have intentions regarding each other except for friendship, Momma."

Confused, her mother's eyes narrowed his way. "M-men don't want pr-pretty w-women for just fr-friends."

"Momma," Carly pleaded, the red back full force in her cheeks. "Stone just cooked us a wonderful meal. Not only that, he fed you. I'm pretty sure you actually like him so no more awkward questions."

"Th-that doesn't m-mean I tr-trust him where y-you are c-concerned. E-Especially as h-he's not an-answered my qu-question."

He'd bet anything Audrey Evans had been a fireball during her heyday. Stone smiled. "I like Carly, ma'am, but as far as my intentions, at this point in our relationship, we are truly friends. We've never held hands or kissed or any of those things couples do who are more than friends."

Which was mostly true. He had brushed that kiss against her hairline, but that hadn't been a real kiss.

He could just as easily have brushed that temple kiss across his sister's forehead. Not true. That kiss should have been innocent, but nothing about touching Carly felt innocent. The brief brushing of his lips against her temple had lit a few fires.

"I do agree that your daughter is beautiful," he continued, holding Carly's mother's gaze. "And I'll admit I wanted to date her. I asked her out on more than one occasion, but we've decided to be friends."

Audrey didn't look convinced. "In-in hopes it w-will lead to s-something m-more?"

Stone's answer was quick and sure. "I wouldn't be opposed, but consider it a privilege to be your daughter's friend."

"Y-you have my bl-blessing to v-visit our h-home any t-time."

"Mom!"

"Deal." Rather than stick his hand out to shake on it, Stone placed his hand over Carly's mother's on the armrest of her wheelchair. "Is tomorrow evening too soon? Or would that be pressing my welcome too far?"

CHAPTER EIGHT

TOMORROW? CARLY'S EYES WIDENED. Maybe her jaw dropped, too. What was Stone thinking?

What was her mother thinking?

No doubt she was having visions of those grandchildren she'd mentioned the other night. Carly's cheeks were so hot they might burst into flames.

"You said you'd be in surgery tomorrow," Carly reminded him, feeling a little surreal.

Stone shrugged. "I was in surgery today. That doesn't stop me from having a life."

Panic filled Carly. She wasn't sure she was mentally, emotionally, or physically prepared to deal with Stone a third night in a row.

Because her responsibilities did keep her from having a life.

A stab of guilt hit her. Not true, just…not true.

"I'm not sure you coming by tomorrow is a good idea," she began, hoping he'd understand he overwhelmed her.

With little effort, he'd topple the precariously held together bits and pieces of her life.

"Th-that's no w-way to sp-speak to a fr-friend," her mother scolded. "Stone i-is w-welcome."

Her mother smiled toward Stone and Carly knew for sure she was having visions of wedding bells and grandkids in her near future.

Please don't think that, Momma.

Whatever Stone's reasons for being there, happy ever after wasn't one of them.

Maybe there wasn't any such thing as happy ever after. Certainly, her mother had never gotten one and Tony hadn't stuck around despite their having planned their future together prior to her mother's illness.

"Y-you c-could c-cook d-dinner for h-him."

Because the way to a man's heart was through his stomach? Was that what her mother was thinking?

Carly didn't want to cook for Stone. She shouldn't cook for Stone. But how could she refuse after her mother's comment?

She was racking her brain as to what she could possibly cook, when he, fortunately, shot that suggestion down.

"Carly has things to do besides cook dinner for me."

Her mother frowned. "Sh-she can c-cook. I t-taught h-her."

Her mother was right. Growing up, they'd cooked and baked together many a night. Never anything fancy, just whatever they were having as their meal. Those times were precious memories.

Happy times that had faded into present reality.

"Mom, Stone isn't doubting my cooking abilities," Carly explained. "He's just acknowledging that I have things to do tomorrow."

"Which is why I'll bring dinner."

Pride had Carly puffing out her chest. Or maybe it was rebellion. "You don't need to feed us, Stone."

"I'd like to feed you." His eyes twinkled and she knew he was flirting, that he didn't care that her mother was watching.

Carly cared. How was she going to explain that he might have an attraction to her, but even under the best of circumstances that would pass.

Carly's life wasn't the best of circumstances.

"L-Let the m-man f-feed y-you."

Carly drew in a deep breath. "First you feed my mother, now she wants you to feed me." Carly shook her head. "You're too charming for your own good."

His grin said he knew it.

Fighting a smile, Carly rolled her eyes. "Seriously, you do not have to bring food."

She would stop by the grocery and pick up a few items just in case she needed to feed him. Something simple, but that tasted good. Things that if he didn't come by she could stretch and make last over the week.

Not that she didn't have enough leftovers in her kitchen to cover a few meals. Still, she could freeze some of the spaghetti.

Carly's mother stayed with them for another ten minutes before fatigue caught up with her. Carly could see the switch flip as her mother's adrenaline surge at having a man in the house faded. Her tremor and speech worsened and she struggled to keep her head up.

"I—I'd l-like b-bed."

Carly stood to push her mother's wheelchair back to her room.

"Can I help you get her into bed?"

"I got this," Carly assured him, waving off his help.

A few minutes later, she maneuvered her mother via the mechanical lift from the chair into her bed. Perhaps she should have let Stone help. Her mother was usually able to help support a little of her weight. But she didn't usually get up out of bed in the evenings to eat dinner. Exhausted, Audrey was a limp ragdoll during the transfer, leaving Carly with extra work in transferring from the wheelchair.

Working as a nurse, she was used to transferring patients, but there was only so much one person could do.

She got her mother into her bed, got her situated, gave her night-time medications via her tube, then sat with her for the few minutes it took her to go to sleep.

Before leaving the room, she bent down and kissed her mother's cheek. "I love you, Momma."

Her mother's lashes fluttered open and she mumbled, "I love you, too."

Her words were so clear, so reminiscent of what Carly had often heard while growing up, what she had felt every moment of her life, her eyes watered.

She stood at her mother's bedside, not surprised when a tear, then another, rolled down her cheek.

Such a good, good woman to be so incapacitated.

Maybe the neurologist would have some miracle cure at her mother's upcoming follow-up appointment.

Which had her questioning how she was going to continue to transfer her mother in and out of the car.

She'd figure it out. Maybe her mother would be having a good day and it wouldn't be a problem. Maybe.

She swiped at her cheeks, dried her eyes, then pasted on a smile as she went to find Stone.

She'd expected him to still be at the small table, but he wasn't. He was in the kitchen, wiping down the countertop. The clean countertop.

He'd cleared the table and done the dishes.

"I won't promise I got things put away in the correct places, but at least there's nothing you have to clean up."

"I…thank you." Carly stared at him, a bit awestruck. None of the boys she'd dated, including Tony, had ever done anything so sweet and unexpected.

Boys. Maybe that was the difference. Stone was a man.

Not that they were dating. They were friends.

"You really didn't have to do that," she continued. "But I appreciate that you did."

"I didn't know how long you'd be. Cleaning up gave me something to do. Plus, I want to help you."

"I could have gotten it after I got Mom to bed. It's not fair for you to cook, plus wash everything."

His smile said cleaning hadn't bothered him in the

slightest. "Like I said, I won't promise things are put away correctly. If you can't find something, just keep looking because I stuck it somewhere."

She nodded.

"Speaking of cabinets, if you have a screwdriver, I'll tighten the screws making that door hang down." He gestured to one of the top cabinet doors that hung at a slight angle.

"I can do that," she assured him. She'd been meaning to for weeks. Every time she was in the kitchen and would see the cabinet, she'd think about it. But there was always something more pressing to get done.

"There's no time like the present. Get me a flathead screwdriver, Carly."

She wanted to argue further, but decided it was easier to get a screwdriver. She dug through some odds and ends until she found the tool in her grandfather's small, rusty toolbox that was stuck in the hallway closet.

Rather than hand it over, she scooted a chair to the cabinet, climbed up, and tightened the loose screws. Opening and closing the door, she made sure her repair had completely corrected the problem.

When she went to step down, Stone put his hands on her waist, steadying her.

Supposedly steadying her.

Because his hands on her waist had quite the opposite effect and she ended up losing her balance and grasping his shoulders as she stepped down from the chair.

"Sorry," she apologized, looking up at him, clinging to his shoulders.

"You should have let me do that." His voice was soft.

"I did just fine."

"You did, but I wanted to help you, Carly. Let me do things for you."

She wondered if his attraction had already waned into

pity. She didn't want his pity. She wanted his…oh, good grief! She wanted him.

Much more than the boys she'd dated in high school and college. Not that she'd slept with them. Just Tony and he'd been okay, a good enough guy, but nothing spectacular when it had come to the act of sex. Definitely nothing spectacular when it had come to sticking around when her circumstances had changed.

"You cooked dinner and cleaned up afterwards," she reminded him. "You've done more than your share of helping."

Why was she still holding onto his shoulders?

Why was he still holding onto her waist?

Why did she want to lean against him, feel his body next to hers?

"I'd like to do more."

Lord help her, so would she, but that thought was futile.

"We've had this conversation. My mother invited you to stop by tomorrow, but please don't bring food."

"Do you want me to stop by tomorrow?"

She should lie and say no.

She should tell him to stay away so she could get her work done.

She should do a lot of things, but instead what she did was realize her thumbs were caressing the man's shoulders. Realized that his hands had slid from her waist to behind her to her low back.

She bit into her cheek and didn't scold herself for doing so. No wonder she was giving in to her nervous tic.

Stone's hands slid up her back in a slow explorative move that she knew she could stop with a single word.

She didn't utter a peep.

When he reached up and pulled the clip from her hair, letting her long locks tumble free, Carly didn't stop him. He dropped the clip onto the countertop beside him, then dug his fingers into her hair.

"So soft," he said, staring at his hands surrounded by her hair. "I knew it would be like this."

"What?"

"Touching you."

"My hair, you mean?"

"Your hair. You. All of it."

"We're friends," she reminded him, not quite believing he was saying the things he was, touching her as if she were...desirable.

"I haven't forgotten."

"Good friends," she added, quoting him from earlier. A shiver ran down her spine, prickling her sensitized skin.

"Very good friends." His fingers tangled further into her hair, then caressed the back of her neck. "The best."

"That feels good," she heard herself admit, perhaps speaking to keep from moaning with pleasure. Stone's fingers were magic. Pure magic.

"Agreed."

At first, she thought he meant touching her felt good, then she realized her fingers were at his neck, were threading into his dark hair, caressing, touching. So, maybe he'd meant her touching him.

Not that her fingers were magical, but she felt as if she had some type of super power when his skin goose-bumped and a low sound emitted from his throat.

Good. If he was doing crazy things to her she wanted to do them back, for him to feel the heart-racing breathlessness too.

Stone lifted her hair away from her neck, bent, and pressed his lips to her throat.

Pinpricks of pleasure covered her skin and Carly moaned.

He nuzzled, kissed, and gently supped at her throat. Carly melted. Her fingers dug into his shoulders for support because she might just puddle on the floor.

"You taste so sweet."

She didn't use any fancy perfumes or lotions. All he could be tasting was soap, water, and her.

He raised his head, stared into her eyes, a thousand questions in his green depths, but one main one that overshadowed all the others.

Rather than say yes, Carly stood onto her tiptoes and answered.

By pressing her lips to his.

Dear sweet heavens. His lips were soft. Perfect against hers.

Perfect in how they moved, in how they tugged at hers, tasted hers. In how he let her explore his mouth, taste him.

Perfect.

Her fingers still tangled in his hair, pulling him closer. His hands slid to her bottom, lifted her into him.

Need like Carly had never known took over every cell of her being.

On and on, they kissed, leaving Carly practically gasping when their mouths separated by a few centimeters. She stared into his eyes and didn't bother to try to hide how dazed she felt. Trying wouldn't have worked. He'd totally overwhelmed her senses. Overwhelmed her.

Trying to catch his breath, Stone rested his forehead against Carly's and stared into the molten honey of her brown eyes. "That was amazing."

Her lips twitched. "You think?"

He laughed. "Afraid you might inflate my ego?"

"I'm quite positive your ego is already inflated."

One side of Stone's mouth tugged upwards. There was no hiding that she was right. Not with her body pressed against him. "It's your fault."

A small smile toyed at her lips. "I can live with that."

Her response surprised him. He'd expected her to pull away once the kiss ended, for her to have regrets, possibly backtrack and ask him to leave. Instead, her hands were around his neck, her forehead was against his, and she was smiling as if she'd enjoyed their kiss as much as he had.

He could only hope she'd enjoyed it half as much.

"I'm going to want to do that again," he warned, watching her closely.

"I figured as much."

"You're okay with that?"

"I'm just trying to figure out what you're going to tell my mother now that you've kissed me."

He grinned. "You think she'll ask?"

Carly's expression twisted in thought. "Actually, I think you'd better run before she asks you to stay forever."

He couldn't quite hold his smile.

The light dancing in Carly's eyes dimmed and concern took its place. "I don't want my mother hurt, Stone. Nor do I want her to have unrealistic expectations. I don't have time to invest in a relationship. Not a friendship or more-than-friendship relationship."

"Because of your mother?"

She took a deep breath, then nodded. "Asking Joyce to stay extra so I can spend time with you isn't an option."

He studied her face, the tension etched into her expression. She believed what she said. Maybe what she said was true. He didn't want to add to her burden, but walking away didn't seem a viable option, either.

Certainly not an acceptable option.

"We don't have to go anywhere, Carly. We can spend time together here, with your mother."

Looking pained, she shook her head. "She'll get the wrong idea."

"What wrong idea would that be?"

Rose bloomed in her cheeks. "That we might fall in love, get married, and have her grandchildren."

This time the but was going to come from him.

"But we'll know the truth."

"None of those things can happen," she agreed.

No matter what happened between him and Carly, and he was hoping a lot would, there would be no marriage, or children. Been there, done part of that, had the deep scars to prove it.

"As long as you and I know the truth, that we're just good friends, we can make this work if you'll try."

Carly's lower lip disappeared between her teeth a moment, then she let out a long breath. "Oh, there's a million reasons, but I'm not sure any of them are enough to keep me away from you."

Warmth filled his chest. "I think I like that."

She blinked up at him. "What?"

"That you want to be with me that much."

Carly laughed, which caused her body to move against his and Stone fought a groan. Her body fit next to his so perfectly, so succinctly, so excitedly.

"Why wouldn't I?" she asked. "You shop, cook, and clean. Every woman's dream man."

"Not every."

That he knew for a fact. Some lessons weren't soon forgotten.

Yes, he had moved on, had been in several decent relationships since Stephanie, but he'd not let anyone get close.

"If things begin to get complicated, we'll go back to the way things were, just work friends," she suggested.

Had she read his mind? Felt the tension memories of the past stirred?

"Sounds perfect," he agreed. "We'll keep things uncomplicated."

Only part of Stone wondered if things weren't already complicated where Carly was concerned.

CHAPTER NINE

"Twister? You want to play a game?"

If Stone had any doubts, the sparkle in Carly's eyes would have convinced him playing a game was just what she needed.

"But there's only two of us. Who is going to spin to tell us what's next?"

"I downloaded an app to my phone that will 'spin' for us. You think I was going to risk you having a reason not to play?"

"I have reasons why I shouldn't play, but—" she glanced at the game he'd gone out to his SUV to bring into her house "—obviously, none of them are enough to keep me from doing exactly that."

"You'll have fun."

"And you?"

"Tangling up on a mat with you?" He waggled his brows. "Yes, I'm going to have fun."

Still smiling, Carly rolled her eyes. "I'm beginning to wonder how old you really are. Ten or in your thirties?"

"I'm not telling," he teased, leaning forward to trace his thumb over her cheek.

"Sorry. Did I have dressing on my face?"

He shook his head. He'd brought them grilled chicken salads, plus had picked up some fresh fruit for dessert.

He held up the game. "I play to win."

"I've noticed."

He arched a brow.

"You don't seem the type to not get your way often."

"More often than you obviously think." His happiness ebbed a little. "That's life. We win some and lose some. It's all good and what makes us into the people we are."

"I suppose." Her smile wavered, too.

Stone grabbed her hand. "Come on. Let's play." He opened the box, read the instructions out loud, then spread the mat. "You ready?"

She eyed the mat then met his gaze. "Sure. Why not?"

He chuckled. "I'm going to remind you later that you were skeptical of my idea."

"You do that."

Stone took out his phone, opened the game app, and put in the settings. Then, he took off his shoes and stretched his arms over his head, then touched his toes.

"Should I be worried?"

He glanced at her.

"You look like you're preparing for a major competition."

"Should I not be worried? Are you a Twister loser?"

"I've no idea," she admitted. "I haven't played since elementary school while at a slumber party."

"Did you win or lose that night?"

Her lips curved upwards. "I won."

"See, I need to be warming up."

Carly laughed and the happy sound vibrated all the way through Stone, leaving him a little wobbly.

"Fine," she agreed, doing some quick stretches of her own. "Prepare to be out-twisted."

He grinned, then tapped the start button on his phone's touch screen. A computerized voice began giving them random instructions.

"Right foot red."

"Right hand yellow."

"Left hand yellow," the voice continued. "Right foot green."

"Hey, that was my spot," Carly accused when Stone purposely chose the spot easiest for Carly to use.

"I didn't see your name there," he teased.

She playfully narrowed her eyes at him. "You know this means war, right?"

He laughed. "Twister war?"

She nodded, placing her left foot on a different green circle at the phone app's bidding.

"Bring it on," he encouraged, purposely stretching beneath her arched body to put his foot on an open green spot on her opposite side.

Laughing and bumping into each other, they continued to play, intentionally tangling with each other as much as possible.

"I'd forgotten how much fun this game was," Stone mused close to her ear, their bodies twisted around each other's to keep their hands and feet on the appropriate colored circles.

"Oh? Has it been a while since you've played?" Carly stretched to put her left hand on a yellow circle, very aware of how her arm brushed against Stone's arm.

"Last time I played was at a college party." He'd not thought of that in years, not until earlier that day while at work, trying to figure out how he could get Carly to relax, to laugh, have fun without their leaving her house.

"Were you much of a partier in college?" she asked as they bumped against each other to put their right feet on different blue circles.

"I partied my share, but was never a diehard partier if that's what you're asking." He'd always felt he had a good balance of fun and hard work in his life. Apparently, Stephanie hadn't thought so. "What about you? Were you a partier in college or were you taking care of your mom then, too?"

Carly put her right foot on the called-out green circle, trying to focus on their conversation and not how her body rubbed against Stone's.

"I had a great high-school experience. Most of my college days were good, too. Mom didn't get so ill until my senior year. Even then, she didn't require around-the-clock care, but just had reached the point she could no longer work and was in a financial mess. I moved home to help with expenses and drove back and forth to university."

Carly and Stone both shifted to put their left feet on yellow circles.

"That couldn't have been easy, working, going to nursing school, and taking care of your mother."

"It wasn't bad." She truly sounded as if it hadn't been. "I loved my mother very much and wanted to take care of her. I only wish I could do more to help her."

He stared at her in amazement. "Surely you realize how much you're doing compared to what most kids do?"

"Most kids aren't trained nurses. I am. Besides, it's not anything that she wouldn't do for me."

"What are you going to do when she reaches the point you can't take care of her here?"

Carly shrugged. "I don't know. I try not to think about that, to just focus on taking care of her a day at a time the best I can."

His heart ached for her, for what she'd been through, what she was going through, what she would go through as her mother's condition worsened.

"You're the strongest woman I've ever met, Carly Evans."

Her gaze jerked to his. "Then you've not met very many women, because I'm a mess and feel as if I'm barely keeping all the plates in the air most days."

He didn't argue with her, just decided they'd had enough serious talk. When the phone app announced right hand yellow, he reached around her to put his hand on the circle. In the process his body bumped up against hers, just hard enough to make her wobble.

"Hey!" she accused. "I'm on to you, trying to distract me with talk, and then knocking me off my feet."

"You're still on your feet," he pointed out.

She was. How she'd managed to stay balanced, he wasn't sure, but she had.

"No thanks to you."

The app said left foot green. Before Stone could move, Carly bumped him with her bottom hard as she maneuvered her left foot onto the green circle.

"Oops, sorry," she said when he wobbled a little, barely managing to keep from falling.

Her eyes danced with amusement.

"Uh-huh. You're going to be."

She laughed. "Probably."

"Right foot blue."

They both moved hard against each other, trying to get to the closest blue circle. Carly made it first and Stone shifted his body to where he put his foot on the blue circle to her other side.

The position had her bottom cradled against him. It was all he could do to fight his instant reaction.

He forced sobering thoughts into his head, thoughts that would hopefully kill his physical response.

When the app called out their next move, Carly wiggled her body against him as she stretched to touch her right hand to a different yellow circle.

He groaned.

She wiggled again.

"Right hand yellow," she reminded him when he didn't move.

He leaned over her and pressed his chest to her back as he slapped his hand on the yellow circle to her right.

He felt her gulp, was glad that the touch of their bodies caused a physical reaction within her, too.

"Left hand yellow."

Carly stretched to put her hand on a free circle. The only other free circles were two to the far left and one to the far right. Stone went for the far right and did so by looping his left arm underneath Carly's body, allowing him to encircle her torso in a hug of sorts.

"Stone!"

"Sorry, it was the easiest to get to."

"Right."

In their current position, he couldn't see her face but could hear the joy in her voice. He hugged her tighter.

She wiggled her bottom.

"Sorry, I have an itch," she teased.

"I could scratch that for you."

"I bet you could."

"Right hand blue."

They both reached for a blue circle and both lost their balance, tumbling to the floor in a heap of laughter.

Stone rolled, pulling Carly with him so that she rested on top of him rather than vice versa.

Smiling with a carefreeness he'd not seen before, she stared down at him. "If I'm on top does that mean I win?"

Stone groaned. "I don't think you could convince me that you being on top means I'm the loser."

She giggled, then dropped her gaze to his lips. "Maybe we could call it a tie for first place. Then, we'd both be winners."

He arched his neck, bringing his mouth within centimeters of hers, stared into her pretty brown eyes. "I'm good with being tied with you, Carly. In a game, with a rope..."

"You're bad, Stone," she whispered against his lips.

Liking the feel of her pressed against his chest, Stone laughed. "Sometimes."

Smiling, watching him closely, Carly rested her weight on his body, placed her hands on his cheeks.

"Am I too heavy for you?" she asked.

He snorted. "Not even close."

"Good." She closed the small gap between their mouths, gently placing her lips against his.

Stone's stomach turned inside out. His hands automatically went to her low back. Every nerve cell in his body overflowed with testosterone and need for this woman.

For Carly.

Any hopes Stone had had of preventing the hardening in his groin were gone.

All from a sweet, light brushing of her lips against his.

Or maybe it was what shone in her eyes as she stared into his.

The way the color had gone to molten honey, to how he watched her inquisitiveness morph into feminine need. Watched as her gaze filled with desire.

For him.

Despite the boiling need bubbling beneath their surfaces, the kiss stayed slow, explorative, full of questions, full of promise.

Right up until Stone could stand it no more and flexed his hips, pressing against her pelvis in an instinctual move.

"Stone," she whispered, cradling his face with a tenderness that about undid him.

"What do you want from me, Carly?"

She lowered her forehead to his and shrugged. "I don't know. Sex would complicate things and I'm not ready for that complication. I'm sorry."

He moved his hands up her back, caressing her. "It's okay. I don't want you to have regrets."

Her forehead still pressed against his, she closed her eyes. "I'm going to have regrets, Stone. When I go to bed tonight and am alone and this plays through my mind, I will regret lots of things."

* * *

"You're Little Miss Perky today."

Carly smiled at Rosalyn, then shrugged. "Just glad to be alive."

"Uh-huh. A certain handsome surgeon wouldn't have anything to do with that gladness, would he?"

Carly shrugged again. Despite how wonderful Stone had been the past week, she didn't feel comfortable talking about him at work.

Probably because part of her didn't believe he would stick around when her life was so crazy.

Her life was crazy. Crazier than normal.

Because she was getting even less sleep than her normal limited quantity.

Because normally she came home and spent time with her mother, and when her mother wasn't awake, she was working on insurance claims. Every night for the past week, she'd spent two to three hours eating and playing with Stone.

Playing games.

Because every night he brought a new game for them to play.

Silly children's games that had them laughing.

Last night he'd brought Old Maid playing cards. Old Maid.

Was that what she was going to some day be? Had he been hinting to her to hurry up and invite him into her bedroom?

Not that they hadn't kissed in her living room, and kitchen, her front porch, and in her driveway when she'd walked him out to his car the night before.

What did all those kisses mean? That they were friends who kissed?

The man consumed her every waking thought. And a whole lot of her sleeping ones.

Not that she had much opportunity for those.

Nor would she be catching up any time soon. She was behind on the number of insurance claims she needed to have processed. Way behind. If she didn't get with it, she'd have to dig into her tiny rainy-day fund to pay Joyce's salary.

She had to get with it.

Tonight, she'd send him home early.

It would be easier to tell him not to come, but she couldn't bring herself to do that.

Not when it would mean not seeing him, talking to him, sharing their day happenings, touching him, kissing him. Yeah, she wasn't strong enough to tell him to stay away.

Which was why she'd seen him every night the past week.

She always managed to send him home by ten, but doing so was getting more and more difficult because she didn't want him to go.

But if he left by ten that give her from ten until two to work on claims. She'd sleep from two until five-thirty when she'd get up to get ready for work, spend a few minutes with her mother, before Joyce got there. On the days Carly didn't have to be at the hospital, she slept until seven when she'd get up and feed her mother, sponge bathe, dress, and spend time with her, process as many claims as she could, and try to keep from getting distracted by thoughts of Stone.

Not an easy thing to do.

Today was her last day of four days on, then she'd have another three days off. Three days in which she needed to buckle down and get caught up on her claims so her precarious finances wouldn't collapse.

Fingers snapped in front of her face. "I ask you about Dr. Parker, and you totally go into la-la land. Guess that answers my question."

Carly smiled at the too-wise-for-her-own-good nurse. "I guess it does."

Rosalyn's dark eyes widened. "Yes?"

"We're just friends." At Rosalyn's disbelieving look, she added, "But he is a wonderful man."

"Just friends." Rosalyn snorted. "You keep telling yourself that, honey, if it makes you feel better."

"It does."

Rosalyn laughed, then sobered. "Has he met your family? Do they like him?"

Carly fought grimacing. She never talked about her family. Not ever. But what would it hurt to admit the truth?

"He met my mother." See, that wasn't so difficult. "He charmed her, of course."

"Of course," Rosalyn concurred. "His family?"

Not believing that she was opening up to her co-worker, Carly shook her head. "I've not met them."

"Well, like you said, it's early still."

Rosalyn's smile didn't waver as they shared a look between friends.

Friends. Carly's heart swelled a little. She'd become so isolated that, although she had people in her life, she couldn't have said she had friends.

Her eyes misted a little, and Rosalyn seemed to know her thoughts because the woman pulled Carly to her for a quick hug.

"Now, you go get to work. We got patients to take care of."

CHAPTER TEN

CARLY GENTLY LIFTED the dressing off Mrs. Kim's chest and winced. Overnight the wound had gone from non-healing to angry. Red streaked out from the wound and a purulent discharge oozed from the open gap.

No wonder her patient's vitals had so drastically changed. When Carly had stepped into the room to do morning vitals, she'd immediately known something was wrong.

Mrs. Kim had been stable and Stone's hospital progress notes had said he planned to discharge her today. That wasn't likely to happen.

Her temperature had spiked to one-hundred-and-one-point-two Fahrenheit. Her heart pounded at a hundred and twenty beats per minute. Her skin had a sickly pallor and her eyes just hadn't tracked Carly well.

Before calling Stone to report the changes in his patient, she'd wanted to assess the wound.

The sight beneath the bandage explained everything.

Rather than finish cleaning the wound, Carly stepped back, removed her gloves, and washed her hands. "I'm calling Dr. Parker, Mrs. Kim, before we go further. He may want additional cultures."

The woman nodded. Carly pulled her cell phone from her scrub pocket and, heart pounding that she was using the direct number Stone had given her, she called him.

Not sure what to expect—would he be happy she'd called him directly or upset?—she filled him in on Mrs. Kim.

"I just finished a lumpectomy and my next procedure was canceled due to a cat scratch on her forearm. Culture the wound, but don't clean or redress it. I want to see. I'll be up there in a few minutes."

Stone shot a quick wink toward the pretty brown-eyed nurse attending to her patient, but verbally addressed the sickly appearing woman lying in the hospital bed.

"Good morning, Mrs. Kim. Your nurse didn't think you looked so well this morning, and I have to agree with her assessment. What happened since I saw you yesterday?"

The feeble elderly woman shrugged. "I got weak."

"Are you hurting?" he asked as he gloved up and moved to her bedside.

"No more than normal," she replied, but grimaced when he pulled away the gauze Carly had used to cover the wound.

Stone wanted to wince himself. Overnight, the wound had reddened and oozed with purulent drainage.

He frowned. "Are you sure that's the same place I checked yesterday?"

Mrs. Kim's tired eyes met his. "That bad?"

"It's not good." He dropped his gaze back to the wound, trying to decide if he wanted to excise it bedside or take her into the operating room. He took off his gloves, tossed them into the appropriate waste bin, then pulled out his phone to call the operating room to check the schedule. He'd had the rescheduled cholecystectomy. Maybe he could slide Mrs. Kim onto the schedule.

"I'm sorry, Dr. Parker, but we're booked solid for anything that's not emergency. Dr. Anderson slid into your canceled slot to do a splenectomy on a post MVA that came into the emergency department."

That decided where he'd be excising the wound.

Hanging up the phone, he turned to Carly. Despite his brain being on Mrs. Kim's wound, his breath caught as he met Carly's brown gaze and she smiled at him.

Breath caught? More like every bodily function halted, leaving him a little dazed.

Gathering his wits, he told her what he planned, what he needed, and then advised Mrs. Kim on what was about to happen.

Carly had done a brief stint in the operating room during her nursing school clinical rotations, but had worked on the medical/surgical floor exclusively since graduation. She loved med/surg. Watching Stone's precise movements as he anesthetized, then opened up Mrs. Kim's wound and cut out infected tissue, she thought she might have missed her calling.

Then again, her fascination might have a lot to do with the surgeon. She'd never seen Stone operate, much less assisted him. The man's hands were steady, skilled, and precise.

While he worked, he chatted with his patient, his voice calm and soothing.

"I'm going to put in a new drain tube then pack the area with antibiotic-soaked gauze."

Carly assisted him as he placed the drain tube.

When he'd finished, he grinned. "Ever think about transferring to the operating room?"

"Once or twice." She didn't elaborate to say that all occurrences had been within the past twenty minutes.

His eyes twinkled and he winked.

Warmth spread through Carly, and she winked back.

Maybe she shouldn't have, but doing so felt right. The happy flicker in his eyes made the whole world feel right.

If only it really were.

* * *

"Momma, it's going to be okay," Carly soothed, stroking her mother's face.

Audrey had gotten so agitated Carly had been forced to give her an injection to calm her down to keep her from hurting herself. Something she'd only had to do on one previous occasion.

Carly cried that night, just as she was crying now.

She wasn't sure what had triggered her mother's outburst, her attempt to get out of bed that had ended with her falling. Carly had barely managed to keep her from crashing to the floor.

The fall had upset her mother worse. Audrey had scrambled to try to get up, scratching Carly several times in the process.

Which had never happened before.

Yes, her mother had spells where she didn't know who Carly was, but she had never been aggressive or violent.

"Oh, Momma," Carly sighed, continuing to stroke her mother's face. The injected medication had almost instantly kicked in, calming her, making getting her back into her bed almost impossible.

With a lift belt, the lift machine, and a lot of maneuvering, Carly had managed, but felt the price in her back, neck, and shoulders.

Then there were the scratches on her face and arms. Scratches that stung from the salty tears streaking Carly's face.

Her mother would be mortified if she knew what she'd done. In her right mind, Audrey wouldn't hurt anyone, much less lash out. The woman who'd flayed at her hadn't been in her right mind. She'd been lost and desperate.

Carly leaned forward, resting her head against her sleeping mother's. "Oh, Momma, I'm sorry this is happening to you."

Then the dam broke and the silent streaks of tears became a torrent onslaught. Sobs racked Carly's body.

When her tears had dried, she went to the bathroom, cleaned her face, then called her mother's neurologist. He'd see her later that week.

The previous time this had happened, he'd adjusted medication and that had seemed to help as there hadn't been another episode until the one that afternoon.

Sighing, Carly stared at her reflection in the mirror. She had bags under her eyes. No wonder. She'd sat up until almost four that morning working on insurance claims. She had to get caught up. She had bills looming over her head and if the neurologist changed her mother's medications, who knew what that would cost?

Her mother had awakened just before seven and Carly had started her day over.

Actually, she'd started her night over.

Her night's work, at any rate.

Somehow she'd not processed her claims correctly the night before and none of her work had been saved. Somehow? Exhaustion and distraction would be how.

She had to get her head on straight.

Carly had wanted to throw up and had felt as if she might. Add in that Audrey hadn't known who Carly was, was convinced she wanted to hurt her and that she needed to escape, all equaled a rough morning.

That her mother had turned violent in her attempts to get away from Carly, that she'd had to turn to medication to calm her mother, struck deep.

A straggling tear slid down Carly's cheek and she swatted it away.

No matter. There was nothing she could do about any of it at this point except to move forward. To stay on task and make the best of what was left of the day. Her mother was asleep and likely would be for several hours, courtesy of the injected medication.

Carly had a lot of work to get done before Stone arrived.

Her gaze met her own in the mirror, took in the dark circles beneath her red-rimmed eyes. Her face was puffy, probably from her crying bout, but maybe from lack of sleep.

"What are you doing, Carly?" she asked herself, not bothering to answer because her answers would accomplish nothing but more stress.

Plus, if she started asking herself questions and answering them, she might have to make an appointment for herself with her mother's neurologist, too.

She shouldn't see Stone that evening. It would take her a big portion of the day to finish the messed-up insurance claims. She needed to get many more than just those done before going to bed tonight. She had bills to pay. Joyce's wages to pay.

Even as she thought it, she knew that when Stone showed up she would stop what she was doing and would spend a few hours basking in his attention.

After all, she had to eat.

And smile.

The man made her smile and right now that seemed like something only a miracle worker could achieve.

Stone was a miracle worker and impossible to ignore.

She would make this work. Maybe she should tell him about the insurance claims.

Why hadn't she?

Pride? Not wanting him to know exactly how financially strapped she was? It wasn't as if he couldn't look around her home, her life, and tell.

Or was it that she didn't want to admit to how guilty she felt that, rather than working on the claims as she needed to be doing, she snuck a few hours a day to spend with him?

Did that make her a bad person? A bad daughter?

The reflection in the mirror didn't answer, just stared back with glassy, red-rimmed eyes.

* * *

"Hello, gorgeous." Stone bent and dropped a kiss on Carly's cheek before walking over to the table to put down the bags of take-out he'd brought with him.

"Obviously, you didn't look at me."

He turned, ran his gaze over her from head to toe. She wore her usual home dress of T-shirt and yoga pants. Her hair was pulled back in its usual ponytail. Her face was make-up-free. She looked tired, her expression pinched, a little haunted.

But the most obvious reason she'd made her comment had to be the scratches across her left cheek.

Scratches that must have been made by her mother. He'd not seen Audrey during a bad spell, other than a few nights that she hadn't known who he or Carly was. Today must have been a bad day. His heart ached for Carly.

He reached out, took her in his arms, and hugged her. "I looked. I liked. I agree with my original statement. You are gorgeous."

Resting her head against his shoulder, she snorted. "You're delusional."

"I do feel that way sometimes when I hold you like this," he admitted, causing her to pull back.

"I knew you'd do this."

"What's that?"

"Make me feel better."

His insides warmed at the compliment. He wanted to make Carly feel better, to make her life better.

"It's probably the freshly baked yeast rolls you are smelling. They smell good enough to make anyone feel better. But I'm good with taking credit for anything that makes you smile."

"Yeast rolls?" She inhaled deeply. "Okay, you convinced me. It's not you." She stepped away from him and began to pull things from the large brown paper bag. "It's definitely the yeast rolls. Yum."

Watching her, he laughed. "Hungry?"

"Starved," she admitted, glancing up as she opened the bread bag and tore off a piece. Her eyes closed and she looked as if she'd just taken a quick trip to heaven. "That is good."

Stone swallowed, trying to clear the knot that formed in his throat. "Remind me to bring you bread every night."

Her eyelids popped open and her gaze met his as she stuck another bite of bread in her mouth. "Sorry. I forgot to eat today. I hadn't realized until just a few moments ago."

He frowned. "You have to take care of yourself or you won't be able to take care of your mother. Then what would she do?"

Her face immediately paled. "You're right. I didn't mean to forget. I was busy and time got away from me."

She didn't need to be skipping meals so Stone was even more grateful he'd brought food.

"You going to tell me about your face?" His gaze lowered, took in the red streaks on her arms. "And your arms?"

She looked away. "I'd rather not."

"Rough day?"

Flinching a little, Carly nodded.

"That bad?" Unable to resist, he reached for her.

"This morning was rough," she mumbled against his chest as she slid her arms around his waist and held him tight, as if she thought she might fall if she let go.

Needing to comfort her any way he could, Stone kissed the top of her head.

"She slept the rest of the day, so I shouldn't be so emotional now." She sighed, then stepped out of his arms and rubbed her hands across her face. "I should be over what happened this morning, but I know her sleeping all afternoon means I will probably have a rough night as she'll likely be awake more than asleep."

Her expression filled with guilt and she moved away from him, removed the last items from the brown paper bag he'd brought their dinner in. "I'm sorry. I shouldn't complain."

Her shoulders drooped a little, as if strained under a heavy load.

"You're not complaining, Carly." Most people he knew would be, would say how unfair life was, would bemoan what she was dealing with. Not Carly. "I asked you about your day and you were telling me."

"It's not what you need or want to hear."

"Not true. I want to hear about you. To know about your life. The good and the bad. Being friends is about more than the good times."

Her gaze cut to him and her lips gave a trembling smile. "Thank you. You are a good man, Stone."

Not that good, but now wasn't the time or place for that conversation. He doubted there ever would be a time or place as he wouldn't want to burden Carly with his problems when she had so many of her own.

"You need me to stay and help with your mother?" he asked as he picked up the brown paper bag and folded it.

She looked at him in surprise. "Why would you do that?"

"To help you."

"Stone, I…"

"We're friends. Friends help friends," he quickly reminded her.

"Like I said, you are a good man. A very good man, but you don't have to do this." She gestured to the food. "Not any of this."

She was throwing up walls. He could almost visibly see them going up between them and he didn't like it. "We've already had this conversation, Carly. I want to do this, to be with you."

She looked torn, as if emotions were battling within her. "Thanks, but I got this. You want me to get you a drink?"

He regarded her a moment, wondered if she'd always felt

the need to carry everything by herself. If pride or strength or conditioning made her feel she had to do this on her own.

Maybe she'd had to and it truly was that she was conditioned to do everything without help. At some point there had been grandparents, but Carly had told him they'd passed before her mother got ill. Other than Joyce, whom she paid, Carly didn't have anyone to lean on.

Which was a sobering thought to someone who had a big family where someone was always sticking out a helping hand.

"I'll take some ice water," he told her, waiting until she'd left to get their drinks before glancing around the room, seeing dozens of things that needed to be done. Things he'd noted each night he'd visited. After how she'd reacted to his offer to tighten the screws on the kitchen cabinet, he'd not mentioned any of the other little things he'd like to do.

"Thanks for dinner, by the way," she said, coming back into the room. "It smells wonderful."

He sat down at the table. "Sure thing. Thank you for the company."

Rather than give her usual response, she just shot him a "yeah, right" look, then asked, "What game am I going to beat you at tonight?"

"You do realize that tying with me doesn't count as beating me?" he teased.

"We didn't tie when we played Trouble, Connect Four, or when we played Old Maid," she reminded him.

Seeing the sparkle he'd come to love in her eyes for the first time since he'd arrived, he grinned. "You won those? Funny, at no point have I felt like a loser."

Carly's smile lit up the small, dingy room that he'd come to feel quite at home in over the past week.

"Sugar-coat however you like," she told him, handing him his water. "But we both know the truth. You just aren't that good at games."

"Or maybe I've been letting you win."

Sitting down at the table perpendicular to him, she regarded him, then shook her head. "Nope. You aren't the type to purposely lose."

"Like I said, I've not felt like a loser."

Except for when he acknowledged that, whether she wanted it or not, Carly needed him and, just like with Stephanie, he was failing her.

Something he intended to rectify.

Carly wasn't going to like what Stone had planned the next evening, but he was determined to help.

Thus, the tool belt and supplies in the back of his SUV. Not that he was a master carpenter, but he'd done enough odd jobs around the house with his dad growing up that he could be handy when needed.

Carly needed handy.

Both her and her house.

After they ate their dinner, he planned to nail down the loose boards on her front porch and around the front porch window. After he got those fixed, he'd sand the peeling paint and freshen up with a new coat.

Grabbing the take-out food bags off his passenger seat, Stone forewent the tools. He'd come back for those when Carly was busy with her mother.

When she met him at the door to unlock it and let him inside, she looked a little frazzled and a whole lot exhausted, just as she had been the evening before.

"You okay?"

"Fine." But she didn't meet his eyes.

His hands were full of their dinner, so he couldn't give in to his urge to pull her into his arms and demand she tell him about her day.

Not immediately. But within seconds, the food was on the dining table and Carly was in his arms.

She let him hold her without uttering a single word of

protest. Instead, she rested her head against his chest and leaned on him as if she was too weary to stand.

Just as she'd done the evening before.

Hell.

"I'm glad you're here," she whispered against his chest.

"Me, too," he said and meant. "Me, too."

He held her in silence for a few minutes, before she pulled away, put on a brave smile, and asked what was for dinner.

"Mexican."

"Yum."

"I hope you're hungry because I brought plenty."

"I see that." She gestured to the bags on the table. "We could invite the whole neighborhood over and not run out of food."

He grinned. "You prefer fajitas or burritos or both?"

She dug through one of the bags, pulled out a tortilla chip and popped it into her mouth. "Let's just spread out what you brought and share."

"Sounds perfect."

Dinner had been perfect. Carly and Stone had eaten, laughed, and for a while she'd completely set aside the stresses of the day.

Unfortunately, they crept back in when her watch alarm went off.

"Sorry, I need to go feed Momma."

"Don't be sorry," he assured her, his eyes compassionate. "I understand."

He seemed to.

Which didn't make sense to Carly. She and Tony had dated for more than a year, had planned to get married after graduating from college. They'd talked kids and forever. Yet he hadn't understood when Carly's mother had gotten more ill, when Carly had moved home to care for her.

He'd been mad. Upset. Jealous. Had accused her of not

having time for him, of not meeting his needs. She'd tried to make time for him, had done her best to make him feel loved and appreciated, but her mother had come first. Tony hadn't understood. He'd left, started seeing someone else, and hadn't looked back.

Neither had Carly.

Not really.

Tony hadn't been the man for her.

Having met Stone, that was easy enough to see.

Not that Stone was the man for her, either, but he'd made her realize there were good guys out there.

Ha. Barely into this "friendship" and she was classifying him as a good guy. Stone was a good guy.

Some day, when she could devote herself to a relationship, she hoped to find a man like him. Because she didn't kid herself by thinking Stone would still be around. He'd tire of her restricted life soon enough.

She bit the inside of her lower lip.

"Thank you for dinner," she told him, trying not to let her thoughts dampen the joy of his being there. "And for the company."

"That's my line," he teased.

She nodded, then went to the kitchen, mixed her mother's meal for her feeding tube and a small bowl in hopes she'd eat some actual food, too, not that she had for the past two days.

Actually, she just hoped her mother was herself and knew her, or even if she thought she was Margaret, Carly's grandmother, that would be okay. The angry woman of the past two days was someone Carly wasn't emotionally ready to deal with again.

It didn't surprise her when Stone followed her into the kitchen, his hands full of the containers their food had been in.

"You can leave that and I'll clean up later," she offered, just as she did every night. Not that he let her, but she offered. Part of her understood his need to be doing something besides sit while she was with her mother. Some nights, she was only gone for fifteen or twenty minutes. Some nights, she'd be in the room with her mother for more than an hour. No doubt cleaning the kitchen gave him something to pass the time.

Why did he keep coming back when she had so little to offer?

"Thank you," she told him again as she picked up the food tray, carried it to her mother's bedroom, and said a quick prayer.

Her mother didn't know who she was, but wasn't as agitated as she'd been earlier. Then again, with the way her head kept bobbing, Carly felt it safe to say that the effects of the calming medication she'd given a second day in a row hadn't worn off yet.

"Momma, I have your dinner."

"I—I'm n-not h-hungry."

"You need to eat." Carly went through their normal routine as she set the tray up next to the bed.

Audrey didn't eat anything by mouth no matter how many times Carly tried to get her mother to. She'd refuse the bite, would push whatever Carly managed to get inside out with her tongue, and had even spit at Carly once, covering her with little splatters. Until all the food she'd made was out of the small bowl and on her mother's bib, the tray, and Carly, Carly had kept trying.

With a sigh, she set down the spoon. "I'm sorry you don't feel like eating tonight, Momma."

Carly flushed her mother's feeding tube, then delivered the high-nutrient mixture. Her mother moaned and groaned as if in pain, saying she didn't want Carly to give her the food, saying she just wanted to go home.

"You are home, Momma." Determined to at least put on a happy show for her mother, not that her mother seemed to care, but maybe her mother was still in there somewhere. "Guess who else is at our home tonight, Momma? Dr. Parker is here. He's in the kitchen. He brought dinner. You have to get to feeling better so you can eat with us again one evening."

She took her mother's hand, held it, kept talking.

"He's been here every night, Momma. He brings dinner, then spends time with me and makes me laugh. I know he's out of my league, that there's no future to us, even he's admitted that, but spending time with him is such a joy." She closed her eyes. "He makes me feel good, Momma. Like my insides are lighter and like the whole world is a bit more colorful just because he's in it. We're friends, but—"

"Y-you l-love h-him."

Carly's gaze shot to her mother's face. Her mother who had said very few coherent things the past two days.

She wanted to deny what her mother said. But what would be the point in arguing with a woman whose mind came and went?

Especially when Carly wasn't so sure that her mother's comment was wrong.

"It's hard not to fall for a man like Stone," she admitted, wondering at how her heart was pounding, knowing she had to say something to take the wedding bells out of her mother's gaze. She couldn't bear to deceive her mother even when her mother might or might not recall the conversation.

"He's a good man, but, Momma, Stone and I aren't destined to be more than just friends. So, don't go thinking anything more. Even if things were different, if I were able to date freely, I wouldn't be interested in a committed relationship. Some day I want to travel and see the world as a travel nurse, to go places and try new things, like what Tony and I had planned to do. The very last thing on my mind is marrying and settling down."

CHAPTER ELEVEN

STONE SHOULDN'T HAVE gone to check on Carly and her mother. Before he'd started hammering, he'd wanted to make sure Audrey wasn't asleep so he wouldn't be disturbing her. From what Carly had implied her mother had been more difficult the past few days. The last thing he'd want was to wake and, possibly, agitate her.

Or overhear Carly's conversation.

But it was good to know Carly didn't want a committed relationship.

Quietly, Stone moved away from the door, went outside to his SUV. Mind racing and muscles tense, he got his tools and the boards he'd brought.

His hammer struck the nail, driving it deep into the wooden plank. Just a few boards tonight, but he had plans to come back on his day off work. He'd work on spiffing up the porch, the paint, maybe even tackle trimming the overgrown bushes and shrubbery. Although there were signs the yard had once been well tended, it had obviously been years, if not decades ago.

Making minor repairs to her home would help Carly regardless of whether she opted to keep the house or to sell it down the road.

After her mother passed and she was free to do anything she wanted to do in life.

She deserved that. The freedom to explore and see the world. He'd done that. In undergrad, he and a group of friends had backpacked Europe, climbed to the base camp at Everest, backpacked in New Zealand, had even gone on a trip to Antarctica. He'd traveled, been free to explore the parts of the world that interested him most, had done residencies in various cities throughout the country and had done several medical mission trips outside the United States. Yes, some of the trips had been about purging his mind of his divorce, but, still, he'd traveled.

Carly hadn't had the freedom to do any of those things, had never been much further than the outskirts of Memphis's city limits.

He wanted her to have that freedom.

Which made him stop to question himself. She didn't want that freedom. Wouldn't choose that freedom. She wanted every moment she could have with her mother.

Even when she exhausted herself and carried the burden alone.

Still, she was grateful for his help even if she didn't really want to accept it.

Was gratitude what had put that light in her eyes earlier? The light that had made him want to toss the hammer down and take her into his arms?

He hoped not, but the notion wouldn't let go.

Just as the notion that Carly needed his friendship more than she needed him as anything more nagged.

If they became lovers, would they be able to remain friends, afterwards?

He hit his thumb with the hammer, cursed, and stuck the pounding appendage into his mouth as if that would somehow help.

He pulled it out of his mouth and inspected the damage. A little red, but no real harm done.

He straightened the nail he should have hit instead of his thumb, then drove it into the board with his hammer.

If he really wanted to help Carly, they should remain just friends.

At the banging noise, Carly excused herself from her mother despite her reluctance to leave her side.

"What are you doing?" she asked Stone, stepping out onto the porch and staring at where he was hammering nails into a loose board.

"What does it look like I'm doing?" He reached into a pouch on his tool belt and pulled out a nail.

"Um…maybe a better question would be why are you doing what you are doing?"

"It needs doing." He positioned the nail, then drove it into place with a few swift hits from the hammer.

"Not by you. It's not your place."

"My repairing a few things while you're with your mother isn't a big deal, Carly," he pointed out in a tone that warned she was overreacting. He took another nail from his tool belt. "Don't make this into more than it is."

It was already happening. His getting bored with waiting while she cared for her mother. She couldn't blame him. He'd been so patient, so kind with her, so much more so than she'd ever expected. Yet she couldn't stop the sick feeling sweeping through her.

"Repairing a few things?" While he hammered the nail, she took in his tool belt, the supplies he'd carried onto the porch, and tried to keep the panic from her voice. "What are you planning?"

"To do a few things around here."

"I don't need you doing things around here."

He didn't look up at her, just kept working. "Sure, you do."

Carly's hands went to her hips. "If you don't like my home, you don't have to come back."

In response, he placed another nail and hammered it into place. Each hit sent a shockwave through Carly.

"Did you hear me?" she asked, when he reached for another nail.

"I heard."

"Then why are you still doing that?"

Pausing, he glanced up. "It's not a big deal."

Her chin tilted. "It is to me."

"Look, it gives me something constructive to do while I'm here."

"You don't have to be here," she reminded him.

"I want to be here."

His words should have soothed the unease in her, but instead had her hands clenching. "Please don't do this. I don't want to be beholden to you."

The desperation in her voice must have gotten to him, because he stopped working, looked up. "You aren't."

"But if you do this, I will feel as if I am."

He stared a few moments, then picked up another nail, checked the railing, and hammered the nail into place, securing the previously loose board. "I can't help your hangups, but you don't owe me anything, Carly."

"That's not fair to you."

He shrugged. "Doing something to help a friend isn't about fair. If the situations were reversed, wouldn't you do the same for me?"

She would do the same for him. More if she could. But...

She regarded him a moment, then sighed. "How am I supposed to argue with you when you make so much sense?"

A relieved grin slid onto his handsome face. "Because you aren't supposed to argue with me. Go finish with your mother, and then come out here and help me."

Still not quite sure what to make of his having come prepared to make repairs on her home, she sighed. "You're going to make me work instead of playing games tonight?"

His eyes twinkled. "I've time for both."

Which made Carly's insides flinch.

He might have time for both, but she didn't. How could she tell him that his being there made her life better in some ways and more stressful in others? She was so far behind with processing insurance claims.

"I…okay, Stone. I'll be back when I can." But rather than walk away, she stood, staring at him, wondering how she would ever repay him and if what her mother had said was true.

Definitely, she wanted him.

How could she not?

He was gorgeous and kind and made her feel alive.

"Go," he told her, breaking into her thoughts. "Because if you keep standing there looking at me like that, I'm going to toss the hammer aside and take you up on what I'm seeing in your eyes."

Carly almost instinctively closed her eyes, but caught herself just in time. She didn't want to close her eyes. She didn't care if Stone saw the truth in her gaze.

Not that she was a hundred percent certain what all that truth actually encompassed, but maybe it was time for her to quit pretending that she only wanted to be friends with him.

When Carly got back to her mother's bedroom, Audrey was sound asleep. Carly flushed her feeding tube, because she couldn't recall if she had earlier or not, then removed the dirty bib and cleaned her mother's face.

Although she stirred, her mother didn't wake.

After a few minutes, Carly gave in to the nervousness flowing through her veins and headed to her bedroom.

Once there, she glanced around, trying to envision the ten by ten room through Stone's eyes. Faded pink walls, an antique full-sized oak bed that had been her grandparents', the matching chest of drawers and oval-mirrored dresser.

A rustic chest that her grandfather had claimed had been his grandfather's where Carly had a few quilts and items from her childhood stored.

Not a setting of seduction or romance for sure.

She walked over to the mirror, took in her tired, haggard appearance, the scratches on her face, and frowned.

Nor was she the image of a temptress.

Ha. Far from it.

Going to the bathroom, she had the quickest shower possible, and once out put on deodorant, lotion, and brushed her teeth. She pulled the rubber band from around her ponytail and her hair fell about her shoulders, long and dark and with a hint of wave.

She pulled on a fresh pair of yoga pants and T-shirt, and then wondered whether she should wear something else. He'd only ever seen her in these, a nurse's uniform, sweats, or shorts, and the clothes she'd changed into the night he'd taken her to Julio's.

Walking to her closet, she opened the door, scooted aside her uniforms, and stared at the remaining bits of her former life.

The clothes seemed as foreign to her as if they'd belonged to someone else.

They had belonged to someone else. She felt nothing like the young woman who'd worn fun, fashionable clothes to class and to the social events she and Tony had attended.

Flashes of memories of concerts down by the Mississippi River, of watching the local sport teams play, of hanging on Beale Street with nothing more to do than go from one club to the next visiting with friends and laughing without a care in the world.

Then everything had changed.

It hadn't really been sudden, just that Carly had been in denial of how bad her mother's disease had progressed until her mother had been forced to quit work and confessed what a financial mess she was in.

Carly had begged out of the apartment she'd shared with three girls, moved home, and taken over the bills.

Taken over everything.

And not looked back.

Until Stone.

She reached out, fingered a pumpkin-colored shirt that had once been one of her favorites. She'd always gotten compliments on how it brought out the coloring of her eyes, skin, and hair, when she wore it.

Maybe she should put it on.

"You don't need to do that."

Carly spun. Stone stood in her bedroom doorway, watching her.

"Sorry, I would have called out, but I didn't want to wake your mother."

"I, uh, that's fine." She glanced back toward her closet, thinking she'd taken too long in trying to decide what to do.

Then again, Stone said she didn't need to change. He was right. For what she wanted, she didn't need clothes.

He leaned against the doorjamb and gave a crooked half-smile.

Carly closed her closet door. "Did I take too long to help you?"

"I finished repairing the loose boards, and plan to start sanding them to apply a coat or two of paint. I came in to get a glass of water, then get back to it. I think I can get most of the sanding done tonight."

She was in her bedroom, had been contemplating seducing him, and he planned to sand?

She regarded him. A sinking feeling settled into her gut. He didn't want her. When push had come to shove, he'd realized she wasn't so tempting after all.

"Stop," he ordered.

She lifted her chin a notch. "Stop what?"

"What you're thinking. You couldn't be further from the truth."

"Then what is the truth?"

He raked his fingers through his hair. "I want you, Carly. A lot. What I don't want is for you to have sex with me out of gratitude."

"You think that's why I…" Embarrassed, she shook her head. "You're the one who couldn't be further from the truth."

"You weren't feeling overly thankful and indebted for my helping you? Because I think you were."

"Yes, I felt thankful for your friendship and your help, but I'm not going to have sex with a man just because he hammered a few nails into my front porch. Besides, from what little I saw, you aren't that good of a carpenter."

He laughed. "Thank you."

Hands on her hips, she frowned. "For what?"

"For being appropriately outraged."

He crossed the room and smiled down at her.

"You want me to be outraged?" she asked, trying to make sense of how he was smiling at her.

"I like your hair like this, by the way. Long, loose, free about your shoulders."

"It gets in the way."

"Of?" he asked, his fingers toying with the strands about her shoulders.

She wanted him to make love to her. Tonight. Now.

The thought hit Carly with the same force as he'd been pounding the nails into the board. They were in her bedroom, he was toying with her hair, and her body was surging with years of pent-up hormones.

She was no seductress. Even with Tony, he'd been the one to initiate sex. But she longed for the knowledge, the prowess, the skills to make this man want her.

No, for him to crave her, need to have her.

Staring at the pulse beating at his throat, she saw him swallow, realized he might be thinking the same thing she was, only was afraid to push because she'd been so adamant that she didn't have time for a relationship. She didn't. They were supposed to just be friends.

Who was she fooling? Just being friends with Stone was impossible.

Not taking whatever he'd give her was impossible.

Acting on instinct, she pushed her hair aside, exposing the curve of her neck, and whispered, "Your lips."

His startled gaze connected with hers. "Carly?"

"Kiss me, Stone. Please, kiss me there." She placed a fingertip on her lips. "Here." This time it was her swallowing. "Everywhere."

"Carly, I—"

"You told me you wanted me," she interrupted, not willing to listen to any arguments he might make. She didn't want logic or reasons why they shouldn't. She wanted him. "You said you wanted to help me," she reminded him, rubbing her palms over his shoulders, slowly and with purpose. "Then help me to forget, Stone. Make me forget everything except you and me. Make love to me like you need me as much as I need you right now."

Stone's brain reminded him of all the things he'd decided while out on her porch.

His brain was no match for Carly's sweet plea.

No match for the raging need that overflowed from him at her words.

Carly wanted him to make love to her, was asking him to do what he desperately wanted to do. The vulnerability shining in her eyes warned that if he turned her down he'd shatter whatever confidence had let her be able to tell him her desires.

Like a fragile butterfly, she was attempting to emerge from the cocoon she'd been hidden in for so long and she was asking him to help her spread her wings.

He felt humbled.

And lucky.

Carly wanted him. Reason left him. Need filled him. Need to give her everything she asked of him.

"No worries about your hair, Carly. It's beautiful, and if it gets in my way, I'll push it aside." He ran his fingers into her hair, nuzzled her neck, felt shivers cover his body. "You smell good."

"I jumped in the shower. I've been working all day, taking care of Mom." Even as she arched into his touch, her voice quivered with a nervousness that made him want to reassure her.

He shook his head. "I don't need to taste soap and water, Carly. I want you on my lips."

"Good, that's what I want." Her fingers dug into his shoulders. "I want to taste you, too, Stone. I feel as if I'll shrivel up inside if I don't have your lips against mine."

He groaned.

Despite how her words thrilled him, he didn't move to her mouth, just continued to explore the curve of her neck, licking and nipping at the sensitive flesh, liking the soft sounds of pleasure in her throat.

His hands slipped beneath her T-shirt, pulled it up over her head. "You're beautiful, Carly. So beautiful."

She mumbled something, but he couldn't make out what, because, gaze locked with his, she reached around and undid her bra clasp and let the scrap of material fall to the floor.

Moving against him, chest pressed against his through the thin material of his T-shirt, she wrapped her arms around his neck, and pulled his mouth to hers and kissed him.

Hard, passionate, full of heat.

Heaven, he thought. That was what she tasted of. Heaven.

Time faded away. The world faded away.

He caressed her, kissed her, put every bit of her to memory.

She touched him with the same fervor, with the same

burning need, as she pulled his shirt off him, stared at his chest with such desire and admiration he wanted to let out a roar of pride.

"How do you manage to look like that and have an impressive brain?" she asked, bending to kiss first one pec then the other.

His muscles tightened to hard knots. "Am I not supposed to be healthy because I have a brain?"

"This..." she trailed kisses down his chest, over his abs "...goes beyond healthy."

"I'll take that as a compliment."

"Yeah, you should, but looking at you makes me feel as if I should put my clothes back on," she admitted, giving voice to her insecurities and bringing out every protective gene in his being.

He cupped her face, forced her to look at him.

"You are beautiful. How many times do I have to say it before you will believe me? Maybe I should show you while I'm telling you." He lowered his hands to her waist, bent to kiss her collarbone. "You are beautiful, Carly." He kissed the opposite collarbone. "So very beautiful."

He bent to the tiny valley between her breasts. Her skin goose-bumped, pebbling her nipples.

His groin strained against his pants.

"You're beautiful, Carly."

"You don't have to keep saying that," she whispered, gasping a little when he kissed her puckered nipple then took it in his mouth.

"I'm going to keep saying it until you believe me." He kissed her other nipple and showered it with attention while running his hands slowly down her sides. He lowered to kiss the tip of her sternum, her belly. "You're beautiful, Carly Evans."

He lowered further, dropping to his knees to stand before her as, holding her hips, he kissed her belly.

* * *

Not quite believing what they were doing, thinking she must be having another fantasy—the best one yet—Carly dug her fingers into Stone's shoulders, whimpered as he brushed his hands over her hips, her bottom, as together they pushed off her yoga pants to let them pool at her feet.

She stepped out of them, kicked them away from where they stood, then rubbed her body against his.

Her thighs clenched at the absolute hardness pressing against her belly.

"Has anyone told you lately how beautiful you are?" he asked as he hooked his fingers into her blue cotton bikini panties to help them join her yoga pants and set about fulfilling his promise to kiss her all over.

Carly trembled, worried her legs were going to fail. She held onto his shoulders for dear life, sure if she were to let go she'd combust from the energy moving through her.

Never had she felt like this. Maybe because Tony had never shown her such complete attention, but she suspected it had more to do with Stone than just how her pleasure seemed to be his number one priority.

The man was an overachiever.

Her body tightened, arched into his touch, and she fought crying out as wave after wave of pleasure rocked her.

"Stone." His name came out husky, sounding foreign to her own ears. Or maybe that was the sound of all those crashing waves muffling her voice?

He leaned forward, kissed the tender flesh he'd just done miraculous things to. "Has anyone told you how beautiful you are?"

"You're crazy."

"About you." Then he set about proving it again.

Carly's eyes closed and she gave up on holding in the sounds emitting from her throat.

Despite her need to hang onto him for support, her fingers refused to stay still, kneading into his shoulders, his neck, threading into his hair, only to grab hold of his shoulders and dig in deep when a heated spasm the size of a tsunami undid her insides.

Stone didn't stop, not until she clamped her mouth closed to keep from crying out.

"Have. To. Be. Quiet," she managed to say between gasps for breath, stroking her hands over his shoulders, loving the strength she felt there.

He stood, kissed her hard, pulled back, and stared into her eyes. "You're beautiful, Carly."

"Stop saying that," she ordered, dropping her forehead against his chin to shield her eyes from his. He made her feel beautiful, made her feel so good, so unlike anything she'd ever known or imagined.

"Never," he warned. "I'm always going to tell you how beautiful you are."

Not always. She knew that. The day would come when Stone would move on to better things, to women who were free to love a man like him, to a woman who could give him all the things he deserved. The thought caused a painful stab in her chest, but he was touching her again and the pain vanished as quickly as it had hit.

For the moment, Stone was hers to touch, to kiss, to love.

So, she did.

His body collapsing against hers, Stone fought roaring with release, fought shouting out that Carly was beautiful.

But her mother was in the bedroom next to them, and although it was unlikely she'd awaken, Stone didn't want to risk it.

Selfish of him, but he wanted Carly to himself tonight, to sleep with her in his arms, to wake her and make love to her again before the sun came up.

She didn't have to work at the hospital tomorrow, but he was scheduled in the operating room at seven.

Leaving her bed wasn't going to be easy and for the

first time ever he considered taking a day off work and just spending the day with Carly.

A short-lived fantasy because he wouldn't cancel a day's worth of surgeries on a whim, but the idea of spending the day with Carly appealed.

"That was amazing," she praised in a breathy voice from beneath him.

Bearing the brunt of his weight to keep from squashing her, he kissed her with a tenderness he didn't recall having ever felt.

Not even with Stephanie, but surely he had once upon a time?

"Hey, Carly?" he whispered against her lips, looking into her glazed-over-with-pleasure eyes.

"Hmm?"

"Anyone told you lately how absolutely beautiful you are?"

Her eyes full of delight, she smiled up at him. "I've heard that a few times lately."

"It's true." More true than she'd ever believe, but he'd keep trying to convince her. He kissed her again. "Can we spend the day together? Not tomorrow, although I wish I could. I'm booked in the OR all day. But the following day? You could have Joyce to stay here. We could go downtown, walk by the river, visit the pyramid, whatever you wanted to do."

The light in her eyes dimmed and she shook her head. "It sounds lovely, but you know I can't."

"Joyce would say yes if you asked her. I would pay her, Carly."

She tensed. "I wouldn't let you."

"Why not? I'm the one who wants her to stay," he pointed out, hoping she'd see things his way. When she remained tense, didn't say anything, he relented. "We can stay here if that's the only way you'll say yes."

Her tension didn't ease. Instead, she wiggled, indicating she wanted free from under his body. Stone rolled off, propped himself up on his side and watched as she put her T-shirt back on.

Once in her panties and T-shirt, she faced him. "I told you from that very first night that taking care of my mother came first, that asking Joyce to stay extra wasn't an option."

"Because you're so independent and stubborn."

She shrugged. "Maybe, but it's the way things have to be."

"Because?"

"Because it's the way things are."

"The way you choose things to be."

Her gaze narrowed. "I didn't choose this, Stone. Nor did I want this, any of this. I warned you from the beginning, told you I wasn't free for a relationship. You are the one who pushed."

He sat up, took her hand into his before the situation got out of control. "Somewhere this conversation took a turn it wasn't meant to take. I want to spend time with you, but am okay if that time is here or somewhere else. I was making suggestions on ways for us to be together."

Pulling her hand free, she got her yoga pants, put them on, then took a deep breath. "I appreciate that, but it would be better if you didn't."

He frowned. "Better for whom?"

"Me. You. My mother."

He sat up on the side of the bed, searched for his T-shirt. "You think my being here is bad for your mother?"

"It's not good for her."

"That's not what you thought the night I cooked spaghetti," he reminded her. "You said she ate better for me than she had in weeks. You should let me help you more."

She closed her eyes, took a deep breath. "You should go."

"No."

Her eyes widened.

He moved across the small room to stand in front of her. "That came out a bit rougher than I meant, but, no, Carly, I'm not leaving. Not like this. I don't know how things changed from fantastic to tense, but I'm not leaving until things are right between us."

She didn't look at him; her shoulders sagged. "I probably just got overly emotional. I've not had sex in a long time."

"How long?"

She didn't meet his eyes, but admitted, "Over five years."

Five years. She'd been celibate five years. Because she thought she couldn't have a life and take care of her mother, too? Or because she'd not been interested in anyone?

"It's been a while for me, too," he admitted. Despite going a little crazy with one-night stands immediately after his divorce, he'd settled into a place where sex for the sake of sex hadn't appealed.

At the jerk of her gaze to his, he continued, "Not five years, but it has been a while, Carly."

"Why?"

"Why haven't you had sex in over five years?"

Her gaze narrowed. "You know exactly why."

"Your mother?" He shook his head. "Not a good reason."

Her jaw dropped. "How can you say that?"

"Because it's true. Your mother is just as ill right now as she was this morning and last week and a month ago. Yet, tonight you had sex. Why?"

"Because…because you were here."

"Because I pushed you to let me in."

"I don't understand what your point is."

"You've held the world at bay for the past five years, not let anyone in. That's why you've not had sex until tonight."

"Obviously letting you in was a mistake."

Her words struck him with the force of a hot poker, slicing deep into his chest. "Do you mean that?"

She closed her eyes, then opened them slowly and shook

her head. "No. I wanted you here tonight, last night, every night you've been here."

"Good, because I don't want you to regret having let me in." He reached out, brushed a strand of hair away from her face. "I'm sorry for upsetting you."

"I'm sorry I got upset. I… I've only been with one man and our relationship was nothing like mine and yours." She took a deep breath. "This is complicated, you know. Our friendship wasn't supposed to get complicated."

"Sex has a tendency to do that."

"Where do we go from here?"

"Nothing's changed, Carly. We're friends, good friends, remember?"

She didn't look convinced.

Stone understood. Despite his words, he wasn't convinced, either.

Everything had changed.

CHAPTER TWELVE

THE BUZZER GOING off indicating that her mother had woken up shouldn't have been a good thing, but Carly welcomed the sound of pending escape.

"I've got to check on her."

Stone nodded, but Carly knew he didn't understand. No one did.

How could they when they didn't live her life?

She started to suggest he go home to get some rest, but he beat her to the punch.

Which didn't really make her feel better.

"I've got to be in the operating room at seven," he told her, searching out the rest of his clothes. "I'll bring dinner when I'm done with my day."

"I have to take Momma to see her neurologist."

"You'll be back before dinner time," he pointed out.

"You don't have to bring dinner," she reminded him, watching as he pulled his underwear, then jeans, on over his lean hips. Totally unfair how hot the man was in a pair of jeans and bare-chested.

What was wrong with her that she was getting hot under the collar so quickly after having been totally satisfied?

Or was that part of the issue? Now she knew what was beneath his scrubs? What he was capable of? That she was getting too attached, too dependent, too used to having him in her life?

Tony had been in love with her, or so he'd claimed for the year before her mother had gotten so ill, and he'd not stayed. She really couldn't expect Stone to stick around when her life was so crazy.

Yes, the past week, they'd made it work, but at what price?

She'd barely slept, her mother kept getting worse, and she'd made more mistakes on her insurance claims than she'd ever made previously all combined.

Even if Stone stuck it out a while longer, she couldn't keep this pace up.

"I know I don't have to," Stone interrupted her thoughts. "But I want to bring dinner and to see you."

His eyes flashed with something she couldn't read, something intense and that warned he wouldn't argue the subject any more. "I'll see you tomorrow evening."

"I think it's time you consider alternative options."

Carly stared at the neurologist, hoping he was going to suggest a treatment that was highly successful.

"Have you checked into any nursing facilities?"

The skin on Carly's face shrunk, pulling tightly across her forehead and cheeks.

"No." She glanced toward where her mother sat in her wheelchair, hating that her specialist broached this subject in front of her, rather than in private. Audrey's eyes were closed and her head slumped over as if she were asleep, but who knew if she was hearing their conversation? "Momma is doing great at home," she assured him, making sure she spoke clearly so if her mother could hear, she'd know Carly had no plans to institutionalize her.

"Is she?"

Carly thought over the past few weeks, at the rapid decline in her mother's health, that she was having so many more bad days than good. "You think she's not?"

"You called and asked for this appointment, Carly.

Why?" He leaned forward, took Carly's hand and gave her an empathetic squeeze. "I think you're doing the best you can, but your mother needs more than what you can do."

He was wrong.

"As in what?" she asked, having to force herself to keep her voice calm. "She has constant attention, has had minimal bedsores, definitely a much lower statistical number than the average bedridden person in a nursing facility." She began tossing out statistics. "She has a one-on-one nurse at her beck and call twenty-four hours a day. She isn't going to get that at a nursing facility."

Dr. Wilton held up his hand to stop her rant. "I'm not saying you aren't providing excellent care. You are. But you aren't a nursing facility meant to provide around-the-clock care for a dying woman."

Carly gasped at his adjective. "Don't say that."

He gave a pointed look, one that was full of empathy and pity and a need to fulfill his professional duty to lay out the facts as he saw them.

"Your mother may live years, but, statistically, she isn't going to be with us much longer. Deep inside, your nursing experience will have taught you that."

He was wrong, again. Her nursing experience had taught her that miracles happened all the time.

"She's just had a few bad days, that's all."

Dr. Wilton sighed. "I can't tell you what to do, but my recommendation remains the same. I feel the best thing is for your mother to be admitted to a nursing facility."

"I disagree and I'm not willing to do that."

As if he'd known that was what she was going to say, he slowly nodded his head back and forth. "What you're doing is admirable, but not in your best interest."

"This isn't about me. It's about what is best for my mother. If you can honestly tell me she will get better care in a nursing facility, then I'll give due consideration to your recommendation. But you can't tell me that because you know I am a trained registered nurse who has the skills to provide my mother with the care she needs in her home where she is going to feel safest and most comfortable. We both know dementia worsens when the environment changes. Moving to a nursing facility might rob her of the few good days she has. I won't do it."

His expression somber, he regarded Carly long moments, then shrugged. "Then let me call in hospice care to help you."

Hospice? Had he lost his mind?

"No. She doesn't need hospice care."

"I didn't say she did."

Ouch. Carly winced. "You think I need help? That this is killing me?" She glared at the neurologist. "I don't find that funny."

"I wasn't trying to be funny. I'm being realistic, using logic instead of emotion, which you aren't able to do due to the circumstances. If this were someone else, you'd advise them the same as I'm advising you."

"I wouldn't," she denied—not if she knew they were doing all that could be done.

"At least think about what I've told you." He printed out a prescription. "This is the new dosage for your mother's medication. I hope it works miracles, Carly. For your sake as much as your mother's."

Carly dropped the prescription off at the pharmacy, sat in the parking lot with her mother for forty-five minutes while waiting for the call that the prescription was ready, then drove back through the drive-through.

"That will be…" The clerk named a price way above what Carly was expecting.

"That much? You're sure? Did her insurance pay anything?"

The woman shook her head. "I'm sorry, but that's what took so long. The pharmacist contacted your mother's doctor about a prior authorization on the medication. Unfortunately, her prescription plan still denied coverage." The woman gave Carly an empathetic look. "Do you want to wait about filling it? Or I could call Dr. Wilton back and see if he could change the medication to something else, something covered by her insurance."

Her mother had already been on all the Parkinson's medications her insurance covered, was still on a few of them.

Carly glanced over at her mother, at the constant tremor, at her glazed-over look that said she just wanted to be in her own bed rather than in the uncomfortable car seat. Carly would like to have taken her mother home rather than her having had to wait to pick up the medication, but she couldn't leave her mother alone.

Nor could she easily buy this new medication.

But what if this was the dose that would make a difference? That would give her more good days?

Carly sucked in a deep breath, mentally figured her bank account, her incoming bills, and knew she was emptying her rainy-day fund with her next words, but said them anyway. "Ring up the prescription. I'll pay for it out of pocket."

The woman nodded, as if she'd known that was what Carly would say. "There is a manufacturing coupon that knocks off fifty dollars. I'll print and apply it for you."

"Thank you," Carly said, thinking she might throw up at how she'd just spent her meager savings. How could a medication cost almost four figures for a mere month's supply, anyway? That it did just seemed ridiculous.

Ridiculous, but still a fact.

She had to get caught up on her insurance claims. Already her next check was going to be a lot less than its usual amount thanks to how much time she'd spent with Stone rather than working.

She'd not done even half her usual number of claims.

She'd barely been maintaining her financial balancing act and this had tipped the scale.

No—spending time with Stone, not doing her work,

being distracted from her work, that was what had tipped the scale.

She couldn't afford to keep seeing him.

"How did your mother's neurology appointment go today?"

Carly winced. She didn't really want to think about how the appointment had gone.

Her mother was always exhausted after an appointment and had passed out in the car. Sleep had been a blessing while they'd waited at the pharmacy, and again after Carly had gotten her settled back into her bed.

Moments after which, Carly had had a good cry.

Or was that a bad cry?

Whatever, she'd sobbed for a few minutes. At Dr. Wilton's recommendations. At the cost of her mother's medication. At the fact that she had just enough money left to cover the house payment, car insurance, electric and water, and almost enough to cover Joyce's salary.

But not quite.

She calculated how many claims she'd need to process over the next few nights to keep everything afloat. Actually, today was the last day of the next two-week pay period. Tonight's claims had to be done. Every last one of them. Plus a few more. With no mistakes. She could do it.

If she could get the claims done, with the extra ones, she could just barely make Joyce's salary. And if a single unexpected expense popped up, she'd sink.

But she wouldn't let that happen. She'd made things work this long, had been doing just fine until Stone had stepped into the picture. Now, she just felt exhausted by it all.

Or maybe she was exhausted because after Stone had left the night before, she'd not been able to sleep. She'd kept reliving his coming to her room, his making love to her, the magic he'd spun. Over and over in her mind, she'd replayed his touches, his kisses.

Her mind had raced, making sleep impossible. So, she'd sat in her mother's room and, as much as her distracted mind and body would allow, worked on insurance claims. She'd gotten very few done.

At some point after five a.m. she'd fallen asleep sitting in the chair and had awakened achy and stiff to her mother moaning and crying.

Caring for her mother in a demented state was bad enough; witnessing her in pain was something Carly could barely bear.

Dr. Wilton thought she should put her mother into a facility. No. Just no.

"It went," she answered Stone's question rather vaguely, reaching up and rubbing her tense neck muscles.

What else could she say? That her mother would likely sleep the rest of the evening and not wake until sometime after midnight, if then? That Carly wanted to crawl between her sheets and sleep for hours on end, too, but would instead sit up most of the night working on the insurance claims she hadn't gotten done?

Insurance claims she had to process before going to work in the morning. She had to meet that quota. Not doing so wasn't a choice.

Not if she wanted to pay Joyce.

Plus, she'd need to leave for work a little early to take the blood and urine Dr. Wilton wanted her to collect on her mother to the hospital lab in the morning and still be able to clock in on time.

A heaviness settled onto her shoulders, making her neck hurt worse than it already did from sleeping in the chair, transporting her mother, and the day's stresses.

Stone had just arrived at her house, was unpacking the food he'd brought for their dinner, and putting hers in front of her, but she'd have to ask him to leave. Soon.

"That good, huh?"

Wishing she weren't a Debbie Downer, especially considering the night before, what they'd shared, which seemed like months ago instead of mere hours, she shrugged. "He wants to see Momma back in a week."

Taking a bite of his Greek salad with grilled chicken, Stone studied her. "Did he say why?"

"To go over labs. Re-evaluate how she's responding to a medication he gave her a new dose of today." She told him the name of the new Parkinson's drug Dr. Wilton had put her mother on. She started to tell him how much the medication had cost, but didn't due to not wanting him to think her petty. Her mother's health was the most important thing.

"Routine visit, then?"

Dr. Wilton didn't routinely make Carly bring her mother in again that quickly. He knew how difficult it was transporting her. Carly had seen the concern in his eyes when he'd been examining her mother. She'd heard the concern in his voice as he'd retested her mini-mental status exam and her number had been three points lower than her test just a few months prior.

Although how he could knock points off for her not being able to copy the design or write a complete sentence was a bit unfair in Carly's mind. Her mother's hands shook so badly that of course her design had looked nothing like the one she'd been asked to recreate.

Then again, her mother's scores on that part of the test hadn't changed from her previous test. It had been recall items that had further dropped her score.

If they'd tested her on the day her mother had met Stone, her score would have been higher.

With how she'd been today, no wonder he'd recommended Carly do something different.

Parkinson's disease and dementia were such frustrating diseases individually. Together they were heartbreaking and Carly's heart was doing just that.

"Not hungry?" Stone asked when Carly didn't eat and

failed to answer his question. "Maybe I should have checked with you to make sure you liked Greek food."

She glanced at the numerous take-away trays he'd unloaded from the bag he'd been carrying when he'd knocked on her door about ten minutes before. She'd been sitting with her sleeping mother, going through insurance claims, stressing about money, and fighting heavy eyelids.

"Greek food is great," she assured him, flexing her neck from side to side and grateful the stretching of muscles eased the spasm some. "Thank you for bringing dinner. I'm just not that hungry. Sorry."

"Don't be," he replied, studying her. "I'm worried about you. You need to eat more."

His comment caught Carly off guard. Stone was worried about her? How long had it been since someone had been worried about her?

Not fair, she quickly corrected herself. Her mother had worried about her, still did when she was herself. Joyce worried about her, too.

She was worried about herself.

Or maybe she was just too tired to think clearly.

Either way, she smiled and was determined that she was going to keep smiling for at least the next thirty minutes. After that, she'd ask Stone to leave so she could work, then get a little sleep before starting her early morning hospital shift.

She'd thought about asking him not to come over, but hadn't. How could she when it was the first time she'd have seen him after they'd made love? He wouldn't have understood if she'd refused to let him come over.

Besides she had to eat and Stone fed her. At the rate her finances were going, without him she might reach the point of not being able to feed herself.

"I appreciate you bringing this." She waved her hand toward the feast he'd spread out on her dining table.

"I'm still learning what you like and, until I'm sure, I want you to have options."

"Options are good, but I can pretty much eat anything," she assured him.

"That's not what I said," he corrected, his eyes full of a tenderness that somehow fit as much as the mischievous twinkle she often saw there.

As crazy as her day had been, as crazy as her night would be, she was glad he had come back after last night.

"I want to bring things you like," he continued. "Not things you can tolerate without complaining."

She laughed a little and took a bite of the food he'd put in front of her. A charbroiled chicken that had been marinated with a Greek dressing. "Mission accomplished. This is delicious."

It was. Too bad her stomach was so twisted that putting in food just made more knots.

"That's better." He reached out, touched her cheek, then traced his fingertip over her still upturned lips. "I like seeing you smile."

He probably thought her the most boring, miserable person he'd ever met. She was the most boring person, but not miserable. Not usually. As tired as she was, she was grateful for another day with her mother, for the hope that tomorrow would be a better day, for the hope that the medicine she'd spent her last dime on would work miracles and she'd get her mother back.

She was grateful for the night before with Stone, for his having made her feel so alive, so aware of her body.

The waiting insurance claims called to her. Ugh. She couldn't lose herself with Stone tonight. Not if she wanted to pay Joyce. Not paying her wasn't an option. She couldn't risk Joyce not coming back and she didn't expect her to work for free.

"Sorry." She truly was because, despite the fact that she didn't have time for this, she recognized how good Stone was to her, that he was making an effort. She really did appreciate his doing so. "I'm not the best company tonight." Or ever. "It really has been a long day."

They all were.

How could she explain how bone weary she felt? How every muscle in her body ached with fatigue and from the toll moving her mother had taken? How she had so much work that night that just the thought of it was overwhelming?

She should get started.

When she met Stone's gaze, he was studying her as if trying to figure out a complicated puzzle. She took another bite so he wouldn't think she didn't like her dinner.

"This isn't about last night, is it?"

Meeting his gaze, seeing the uncertainty there, she felt a need to reassure him hit. He was a good man. He didn't deserve her craziness. "I don't regret last night. Do you?"

"Are you kidding me?" he asked. "Last night was amazing. Come on," he surprised her by saying as he stood up from the dining table. He held his hand out. "I want to do something."

Placing her hand in his, Carly arched a brow. Curious, she let him lead her to her small sofa.

"Lie down."

Didn't he know if she lay down she'd be out like a light? She started to argue.

"Lie down, Carly," he repeated, his voice more firm.

Carly's gaze dropped to the sofa. She needed to keep a clear head, to stay awake. Or maybe he meant to… "Stone, my mother is in the next room and there's no door to shut for privacy and—"

The twinkle was back and he laughed. "I like where your mind went, but that's not where mine's at." He waggled his brows. "Not at the moment. But later, after you've relaxed a little, then yeah, I'd like to see if I missed kissing any spots last night."

"You didn't," she assured him, memories heating her cheeks. "I've never been kissed like that."

"Good, I don't want anyone else kissing you that way. Just me."

"They haven't, not even Tony. I..." She cut herself off. No way did she want to talk about Tony, especially not to Stone.

But rather than question her on her ex, he let go of her hand and pointed to the sofa. "Humor me for a few minutes and lie down, Carly. Do this for me."

Curious and compelled to do as he wanted, she lay down, propped her ankles on one armrest, her head on the other.

"Now, close your eyes."

"What?" She frowned. He didn't know what he was asking, how little sleep she'd gotten the past week, but especially the last few nights.

"Do you trust me, Carly?"

She stared at where he stood next to the sofa. Lord help her, she did trust him. She'd never have let him into her bedroom if she hadn't.

"I do."

"Then do as I ask," he ordered in a gentle, but determined tone. "Close your eyes and keep them closed."

Carly closed her eyes, willed herself not to go to sleep, and listened to him move to the end of the sofa. She almost jumped when his hands grasped her shoulders. His brilliant, magical fingers that had touched her all over the night before now applied just the right amount of pressure as they kneaded into her achy muscles.

Dear sweet heavens above!

"That feels good," she told him. "You really don't have to do this."

But don't ever stop, please.

Because his fingers were working the tension out of her neck and shoulders, were working magic through every tight, strained, painful fiber of her body. A different magic from the night before, but that magic was there, too. That magical chemistry seemed to always be an undercurrent between them.

"I feel guilty letting you do this," she murmured, thinking she might go into full-out purr mode any moment. "You worked all day at the hospital. I didn't."

"Somehow, Carly…" his voice was low, as soothing as his hands "… I'm positive you worked harder than I did. Taking care of someone you love who's ill isn't easy."

Something shifted inside Carly. Something sweet and tender and grateful and completely foreign.

Tony had never understood. Not once. That someone as wonderful as Stone did seemed impossible.

"Thank you." Her voice broke a little, but she didn't care. How could she care about anything when her body was going from a tight mess to ooey-gooey butter?

"You're welcome, Carly. Anyone told you how beautiful you are today?"

She smiled. How could she not? "I did get a text saying something along those lines."

"You got that? I wondered when I didn't hear back."

"I was at the neurologist's when it came through and before I could respond, Dr. Wilton came into the room. Then…" Then, she had gotten caught up in what was going on with her mother and had forgotten she hadn't responded. Would he be upset if she told him the truth? "I'm sorry I didn't text back."

"I might question if that was an intentional move with anyone other than you," he admitted.

If Carly didn't know better, she'd think she heard a need for reassurance.

"I'm not into game playing, Stone. I didn't intentionally ignore your text. It was a rough day getting Momma back and forth to her appointment."

"I'm sorry you had a bad day, Carly."

"You being here helps."

It also hurt because she needed to be working. A few more minutes would be okay. Surely. Because his fingers felt so good massaging her tight muscles. His hands felt so good touching her.

"I'm glad this is helping."

"It is. If you're trying to seduce me, it's working."

Whatever she'd thought she'd heard was gone as he said, "I'll keep that in mind for when I am trying to seduce you. This is about you relaxing, on working out the kink in your neck that you rubbed repeatedly throughout what little dinner you ate. Now, be quiet and just enjoy."

It would be difficult not to enjoy this man's hands on her body. His fingers were magic. Magic and wonderful and truly releasing the achiness in her muscles.

She could get used to this, but knew better than to let herself. She'd learned that lesson with Tony.

Not that Tony had ever massaged her neck and shoulders. Not even when he'd been wanting sex had he done anything so giving.

Time with Stone was dangerous and irresistible because he blinded her to everything except him.

What a fool she was.

Maybe she hadn't learned enough lessons from Tony.

No, she couldn't judge Stone from what had happened with Tony. They weren't cut from the same cloth. Plus, she and Stone were friends. There were no long-term expectations.

She wouldn't rely on him and he wouldn't rely on her, because they were temporary.

Why did that thought leave a hollow ache inside her?

CHAPTER THIRTEEN

CARLY'S BODY HAD gone limp over ten minutes ago, but Stone continued to massage her muscles, wanting to make sure when she woke, the tension was gone.

Or maybe he just wanted the excuse to continue touching her. Not as he'd touched her the night before, but a touch meant to soothe.

He smiled at where her mind had gone when he'd told her to lie down. Under different circumstances that would have been exactly why, but exhaustion had been etched on her face. Hadn't she slept after he'd left the night before? Obviously not. Had she been up with her mother or had thoughts of what happened between them kept her awake?

The soft, even rise and fall of her chest confirmed that she'd fallen asleep. Good. She needed to rest.

Stone straightened, then went to the table to clear off the remains of their dinner. She really hadn't eaten much, but obviously she needed sleep more than food. He put the leftover food in Carly's mostly bare refrigerator. Other than her mother's feeding-tube meals and leftovers from the meals he'd brought, the entire house seemed void of food.

Stone got a washcloth and wiped off the small table where they'd eaten, thinking about Carly.

The night before she'd stood at her closet, studying her wardrobe from the past, and he'd seen the pain in her eyes, the indecision and grief for what had once been. He'd wanted to ease that pain.

At the hospital, he saw the person in the photos scattered around this house. Having spent time with her away from the hospital, Stone knew Carly didn't have an easy life despite the easy smile she freely brandished at the hospital.

Other than Joyce, Carly provided all her mother's care. Should he check on Audrey?

Carly constantly went back and forth to her mother's room, even when her mother was sleeping. He quietly entered the room, saw Audrey was still sound asleep.

Despite having been at the house every night for going on two weeks, this room seemed off limits and he'd only been inside a time or two with Carly at his side. He glanced around the small bedroom that was monopolized by the hospital bed. A wooden rocking chair similar to the one in the living room was across from the bed. A plugged-in laptop sat on the floor next to the chair, as did a water bottle with the hospital logo on the side.

Carly spent a lot of time in that chair.

Too much time.

"Wh-who are y-you?"

His gaze shot to Carly's mother and he smiled at the frail-looking shell of the woman from the photos. "Stone Parker. We met last week when I fed you spaghetti, remember? I'm Carly's friend."

She stared blankly. "Who's Car-Carly?"

He knew Carly had been having a difficult time with her mother. But Audrey had seemed very clear-headed on the night he'd met her. The blank look in her eyes told the reality.

"Your daughter. She and I work at the hospital together."

Audrey's eyes closed and Stone thought she'd fallen back asleep, but she opened them and glared. "I-If you th-think sh-she'll t-take you b-back, y-you're wr-wrong."

Stone wasn't sure who she meant, but didn't speak, just

waited to see if she'd say more and hoped she didn't become agitated to where he'd need to wake Carly.

When her gaze met his, tears shone. "D-don't l-leave me a-again."

Her request didn't fit her previous comment, but Stone took her tremoring hand into his. "I'm here, Audrey."

"I—I knew y-you w-would ch-change your m-mind."

"About?"

"Our b-baby. I'm p-pregnant."

She thought he was Carly's father. Stone wasn't sure what to say or do, so he held her hand until, murmuring about their future life together, she fell asleep.

Then he held her frail, shaking hand longer.

Memories hit him.

Once upon a time, he'd been no better than Carly's father. Oh, he'd married Stephanie, had insisted upon helping her, but she hadn't wanted his help or anything else from him.

Yeah, he had some hefty baggage of his own that he didn't think Carly was likely to understand.

Carly woke with a start, letting her eyes adjust to the low light, realizing she'd fallen asleep on her living-room sofa.

What had she been doing…? Stone had been massaging her neck and she'd gone to sleep. Stone. She smiled at the joy that swelled in her heart when she thought of him.

Where was he?

She glanced at her watch, strained to read the time.

Panic hit her. Almost five a.m. Soon her watch alarm would be going off to wake her to leave for the hospital.

She had to draw her mother's labs, get a urine sample even if it meant catheterizing her mother, plus, get to the hospital early to drop off the samples to the lab.

Her mother! She'd not checked on her or changed her adult diaper or given her feeding-tube meal or… Guilt hit her as she jumped from the sofa.

Recalling all the insurance claims she'd not done from the night before, she winced. She needed those claims. No, not needed. She had to have them. How was she going to pay Joyce when she failed to do her work?

What had she done? Gone to sleep as if she didn't have a care in the world. How could she have fallen asleep?

Maybe she could get a few claims cleared out in the thirty or so minutes before she had to jump into the shower. Tonight, she'd have to stay on task and get lots done even if it meant not sleeping. Maybe she could work extra over the next pay period, balance things until that check came in, and somehow not go under. Maybe. After the almost nine hours she'd slept she ought to be rested up enough to pull an all-nighter.

As quietly as she could, she made her way to her mother's bedroom and stopped in shock in the doorway.

The small bedside lamp was on, casting a golden hue around the room. Her mother slept peacefully.

So did Stone.

His large body was stretched out in the rocking chair, his head leaned back, and his breathing even and steady.

He'd stayed? She'd automatically assumed he'd left after she'd fallen asleep.

Why had he gone to her mother's room?

Had her mother awakened and Carly slept through it?

More guilt hit her. How could she have allowed this to happen?

Even worse, how was she going to get her laptop without waking him up?

Without waking him up? She needed to wake him up. He couldn't be there when Joyce arrived. No way.

Never would she be able to explain away his presence overnight.

Yes, she was a grown woman and could do what she wanted, but Joyce was an old-fashioned woman, which Carly loved about her. Her mother's caretaker would not approve of Stone having spent the night, four desserts or not. Plus, there was that worrying-about-her thing that Joyce did—which hadn't she acknowledged the night before was a good thing?

There were downsides to someone worrying about you. Like a responsibility to not do things that made them worry.

She reached out and touched Stone's shoulder. "Stone? Wake up."

Although appearing groggy, he opened his eyes and immediately smiled. "Good morning, Beautiful."

Good grief. First thing in the morning, her highly stressed, and his smile still rocked her world.

Which was scary.

And unacceptable because look at what had happened the night before.

"You have to leave," she told him in as low a whisper as she could with hopes of still being heard. The last thing she needed was to wake her mother.

"What time is it?" To his credit, his voice was equally low.

She told him. "Please. You have to leave. Before Momma wakes and definitely before Joyce gets here."

He stood from the chair and it rocked back. At some point in the night, it had shifted close enough that it bumped up against the wall.

The smack of the wooden chair against the sheetrock wall thundered around the room.

Carly's breath caught. Her gaze shot to her mother, who seemed oblivious that there were two people in her bedroom, making lots of noise.

"Leave. Now. Please."

His brows veeing, Stone followed her out of the bedroom. "What's wrong?"

"You're still here, that's what's wrong." Angry at herself for the situation she'd let happen, she lit into him. "How dare you spend the night at my house uninvited?"

Shock registered in his eyes.

He raked his fingers through his hair. "You fell asleep and so I checked on your mother. She asked me to stay. I fed her and cleaned her for bed, then sat with her. Was that not the right thing to do?"

He'd fed her mother, cleaned her for bed. Carly's heart pounded, thumping "Why? Why?" over and over. Why would Stone do those things?

"My mother asked you to stay?" was what she asked.

Stretching again, he nodded. "I didn't think you'd mind or I would have left, Carly. I wanted to help you so I took care of your mother so you could rest."

Why did she want to hug him and hit him at the same time?

"I had things I needed to do."

He studied her. "Such as?"

She tilted her chin upward. "How I spend my time away from work is really not any of your business."

He stared at her as if she'd grown a second head. "I know it's early in the morning, but I feel as if I'm missing something. I thought I did something good. Why are you upset with me?"

"Because…because…" She struggled to pull out a concrete answer. "Because I don't want you here."

It wasn't the truth, but it was what spewed from her mouth.

"We can't be friends, Stone. We just can't."

"That doesn't make sense. We are already friends."

"That's just it." She fought to keep her tone low. "We're not friends. Don't you get it?"

"Apparently not because I don't understand why you are upset with me. Are you always like this in the mornings?"

"On mornings when I wake up to find a man stayed at my house all night? Yes, I'm upset. And, because you kept me from doing things I needed to get done last night."

He was obviously confused; his gaze narrowed. "Fine.

You're not a morning person. I can live with that and will make a note to let you sleep late in the future. Tell me what things need done and I'll help you this morning. We can knock them out together."

Feeling more and more distraught, partially at the situation she'd let herself get into and partially at how wonderful he was because that was making all this so much more difficult, she shook her head. "You can't help me."

"I'm not a useless person, Carly," he pointed out as if it were news to her. "I have skills and want to help."

"You can't help me." She turned away and wrung her hands. She'd done this. She'd figure a way out of it.

"Carly—"

"Just stop," she interrupted, frustrated by everything about him. "I've told you that you can't help me, so take me for my word. You can't help me." She emphasized each word of the last sentence. "No one can. Just leave."

"But—"

"I need you to leave. Now." She didn't look at him, but could feel his gaze boring into her back.

He must have picked up on her desperation, because after another moment of staring at her he moved closer, turned her around to face him, and kissed her cheek.

"I'll see you at the hospital," he told her. He stopped at the door, his hand on the knob, and turned back to her. "We'll talk after you've calmed down."

The moment he was out her front door, Carly hurried to it, locked the deadbolt, and watched him leave through the little diamond-shaped window panel.

When his taillights disappeared, she burst into tears because this was the last time Stone would leave her home. Because she couldn't let him come back.

CHAPTER FOURTEEN

STONE HAD BEEN in surgery for most of the morning cleaning out an abscess on a patient's leg that had gone horribly wrong and morphed into an infection that might cost the man his leg.

Stone hoped not. He was doing everything he knew to try to save the limb, but the guy's poorly controlled diabetes and decreased circulation weren't helping matters.

Stone rather felt as if he had decreased circulation to his brain himself.

Staying focused on what he was doing had been a mental chore requiring great effort and constant redirecting.

Because he couldn't stop thinking about Carly.

About how she'd looked when she'd awakened him. Wide-eyed, flushed, annoyed, desperate.

She'd been in a panic. Desperate to get rid of him.

"Good afternoon, Dr. Parker," Rosalyn greeted him when he walked onto the surgical floor. "My census shows you've been busy this morning."

He nodded. "Too busy. Is Carly around?"

At his question, Rosalyn gave a knowing smile. "Our manager sent her on break. She's in the staff room."

Perfect. Hopefully, she was alone and they could talk while she ate.

Only, when Stone went into the break room, Carly wasn't eating.

She was frowning at a laptop screen and typing as quickly as her fingers would go.

"Hey, Beautiful."

She jumped at his comment, glanced up, saw him, then, looking perturbed that he'd interrupted, went back to typing. "Not now, please."

Huh? He sat down across from her and watched her work. Her fingers had slowed and when she glanced up, she gave him a pointed look.

"Is there something you need?"

"No."

"Good. Then, if you don't mind, could you go somewhere else?"

"I definitely mind, so maybe you'd better explain this sudden predilection for telling me to leave? First this morning and then, again, now."

Pushing the laptop back, she sighed. "Look, Stone, I don't have time to deal with you right now."

To deal with him? Clearly something was wrong.

"Can I help you?"

"No." Her answer was immediate. Succinct.

"Why not?"

"Because you can't help me. How many times do I have to say that?" Annoyance roughened her voice.

"I'm a man of many talents, Carly. Let me at least try."

She pushed back from the table. "What I need is for you to leave me alone so I can help myself."

Ouch.

"Are you upset I sat with your mother last night?"

"No. Yes." She kept her gaze focused on the computer, but her fingers weren't typing.

"If I did something wrong, I'm sorry."

She took a deep breath, glanced up from the laptop screen. "I'm the one who did something wrong. Not you."

"What do you want me to bring for dinner tonight?"

Her gaze darkened. "I don't want you to bring dinner."

"You want to go out? Can Joyce stay with your mother?"

"Don't you get it?" Her annoyance thickened. "I don't want to see you after work tonight, Stone."

Stone's stomach twisted into a knot. "Why not?"

"I'm busy."

"Taking care of your mother?"

"Among other things."

"Let me help you."

"You can't help. I work a second job, Stone. Only, I've not been working it, because I've been spending too much time with you."

Carly worked a second job? On top of taking care of her mother and having a full-time position at the hospital?

"A second job I didn't do last night and I had an email this morning reprimanding me due to my significantly decreased production over the past two weeks. My boss wanted to know if I was ill." She pressed her fingertips into her temple, rubbing hard there, and lifted hollow eyes to him. "Please just go away and stay out of my life, before you ruin everything."

Her words pierced into Stone. They said history repeated itself. Apparently so. Stephanie thought he'd ruined her life, too.

He stood, pushed his chair beneath the table, and stared at the bristling woman sitting there.

She meant what she was saying. She didn't want his help. She wanted him out of her life.

"I won't bother you again."

Fighting back a dam full of emotion, Carly watched Stone leave for the second time that day. Only, as he walked out of the break room, there was no backward glance.

Good. She needed him to leave, needed to get her mind back onto managing her life and the insurance claims. She didn't usually bring her laptop to work, but had today so she could work during whatever break she got.

She'd made a little headway, too. Right up until Stone showed and got her brain jumping every which way. Her pulse, too.

She dropped her forehead to the tabletop and rolled her head back and forth. Ugh.

Pushing Stone away was the right thing. Being with him had made a mess of everything.

So why didn't she feel better?

Because she'd known better, but had dallied with him too long, and she was going to have to take her juggling act to new heights.

Even worse, she was going to have to bury her pride and ask Joyce if she could pay her two weeks late, something she'd never had to do before and something she'd make sure to never have to do again.

Stone didn't show at Carly's that night.

Carly hadn't expected him to, but thoughts that he might distracted her more than she liked. Her mother had had a decent day with Joyce and had settled in for the night, allowing Carly to get through a fair amount of claims, but not nearly enough to make up for lost time.

For the next week she spent every spare second she had working on claims, foregoing sleep in favor of processing as many as she could.

If she'd calculated correctly, she should have pulled off enough to be able to make up Joyce's pay. There wouldn't be any extra, but she would be able to pay her immediately pending expenses and Joyce's back-pay.

That was enough and she'd count her blessings.

She'd fallen into her old routine: wake, take care of her mother, work, come home to relieve Joyce, take care of her mother, insurance claims, sleep a few hours, repeat.

At the hospital, she saw Stone. How could she not when she took care of his patients? But he didn't smile or go out of his way to speak to her. If communication was necessary, they were both to the point with no pleasantries.

She lost weight. She had no appetite, could barely force food down her throat. Just as well as there had been no money for food beyond her mother's and she'd lived on leftovers and freebie packs of crackers.

"You don't look so good, girl."

Carly gave a small smile. Leave it to Rosalyn to bluntly tell her the truth.

"You and Dr. Parker aren't making googly eyes at each other and you look like you've lost your best friend. Something bad happen?"

Only of Carly's own doing.

It had needed to be done, but letting him go hurt.

She met her friend's eyes, gave a little shrug and fought to keep her tears in check.

"Oh, honey!" Rosalyn wrapped her into a bear hug. "Did he hurt you? I told him he'd better not hurt you."

Carly shook her head. "It wasn't his fault. It was mine."

"Yours?" Still holding onto her shoulders, Rosalyn pulled back and stared. "You did Dr. Parker wrong?"

Carly sighed. "From the moment I ever let him think something could be between us, I did him wrong."

Confusion contorted Rosalyn's face. "Why can't there be something between you? You were both walking on clouds just a couple of weeks ago."

Carly agreed. For a short little bit of time she had walked on clouds. Only clouds had no substance and she'd quickly crashed back to reality.

"I fooled myself into thinking that I could manage my life and have Stone in it, too," she admitted, surprised she was revealing so much. Then again, her co-worker had been right when she'd said Carly looked as if she'd lost her best friend. She had lost him. "I couldn't and we said goodbye."

Rosalyn frowned. "You okay?"

"Not really," Carly admitted, then shook her head to

clear her mind. "I'm fine," she corrected, then went for broke. "It's my mother who isn't. She has end-stage Parkinson's complicated by dementia. I'm an only child, all she has." Her mother was all she had. "I don't have time to devote to a relationship and ended things before it got even more complicated." Was that even possible? How much more complicated could things have been than with her heart and body all tangled up in him?

"Stone deserves better," she added, knowing it was true. He deserved someone who could freely love him and give him all the things he deserved.

Rosalyn continued to look confused. "Don't you think that's something he should decide for himself? Maybe he didn't want better than what you can give him?"

Any sane man would want more than what she could give him.

"You make it sound simple but it isn't. I work. All the time. When I'm not here, I work for an insurance company processing claims. I get paid by the job. If I don't work, I don't get paid. If I don't get paid, I can't pay the bills. There isn't anyone else. I have to do it. I don't have time to have Stone in my life."

"That's a bad way to be in, girl. That man is a good one and they are few and far between. I got lucky with mine. Thought you'd gotten lucky with yours. Didn't know you didn't want him."

"I wanted him," Carly admitted, realizing how much she'd missed having someone to talk to, realizing that, despite the fact that she'd always held everyone at the hospital at arm's length, she'd developed a genuine caring for Rosalyn. "I do want him," she corrected. "I just can't have him and survive. Not financially or mentally or emotionally." She sucked in a deep breath. "I wanted to, but it didn't work. Stone and I both paid the price for my having deceived myself that I could spend time with him."

She gave her friend a wobbly smile. "Even when logic

tells you the truth, it's amazing what you can convince yourself of when you want something badly enough."

"What if he was willing to wait for you?"

At the male voice, Carly spun. "Stone!"

Carly's gaze cut from the handsome doctor standing before her to the African American nurse, who just shrugged.

"I've got work to do and am not needed here," she said, then left the room, leaving Carly and Stone alone.

Heart pounding, Carly soaked in the man she'd been talking about. "I didn't know you were behind me."

"Obviously."

"You really need to stop eavesdropping."

"It seems we've come full circle." His gaze bore into hers. "You didn't answer my question."

"You mean wait until my mother dies?" Her question sounded crass, but wasn't that essentially what he was asking? "That's morbid. I couldn't do that."

"Obviously there's a lot of things you couldn't do. Like tell me the truth, for instance."

"I didn't lie to you."

"You didn't tell me about your second job, that I was interfering in your life."

"I did tell you," she corrected.

"Not until it was too late and you'd pushed me away."

"You wouldn't have listened. I told you repeatedly I didn't have time for a relationship, but you thought you knew better and wouldn't listen," she reminded him. "I... I got sucked into the magic of being with you and it almost cost me everything."

"By my letting you sleep when you were so exhausted you could barely hold your head up?"

"I shouldn't have slept." At his tightened expression, she clarified. "If I don't work the extra job, I can't afford Joyce. If I can't afford Joyce, my mother would have to stay at home alone or go into a nursing facility. Neither of those options appeal. I have to work. When I am with you, I don't work."

Finally seeming to grasp the stark reality of her situation, he raked his fingers through his hair. "You could have told me, Carly. Why didn't you?"

"Tell you I was in dire straits financially and worked two full-time jobs, plus took care of my invalid mother?" She shook her head. "What man would have stuck around for that?"

"Which seems a moot point since you didn't want me to stick around and told me to leave."

"My telling you to leave just sped up the natural progression of our relationship."

"The natural progression of our relationship was that I'd leave?"

"Are you saying you wouldn't have? We both know you deserve better than what I can give you, that you'd have tired of me soon enough."

Not looking away from her, he shrugged. "I guess we'll never know, will we?"

"I guess not." Unable to bear the intensity of his gaze, she glanced at her watch. "Sorry. My break is over. I have to go clock back in."

"Work waits."

His sarcasm wasn't lost on her. He didn't understand. No one could. Not really. She lifted her chin, held her head high, and told herself she was better off without him.

"It always does."

"Joyce, I'm home," Carly called when she got home that evening. She'd worked over an hour beyond her shift, but hadn't minded the extra work. She'd welcomed it. Just as she welcomed the insurance claims she worked on night after night until she fell asleep in exhaustion.

She needed exhaustion to keep her mind off Stone.

Off their conversation.

He wouldn't have waited for her. He hadn't even answered her question when she'd asked if he would have.

Of course, he wouldn't have. He'd have grown tired of coming second to her mother, to her having to work all the time and not being able to meet his needs, to go to normal social functions with him.

"Joyce?" she called again, stepping into her mother's room.

Her mother was asleep, as was the person sitting in the rocking chair.

He wasn't Joyce.

Stone sat in the chair.

What was he doing there?

Stone opened his eyes, saw Carly standing over him. He hadn't meant to go to sleep, but hadn't slept well much at all since Carly had pushed him out of her life.

"What are you doing here?"

"To answer your question."

"What question?"

"The one I didn't answer at the hospital today." He stood from the rocking chair, but didn't move towards her. "I wouldn't have left you, Carly. Not in a million lifetimes."

She closed her eyes. "Why are you saying this?"

"Because it's true. Because I miss you. Because I never really believed we were just friends. I wanted you for myself from the beginning, but when I learned about your mom, I realized you deserved a life without being tied down to someone."

"I don't consider taking care of my mother as being tied down," she defended, crossing her arms, and daring him with her expression to say otherwise.

"I didn't mean your mother," he clarified. "I meant me."

What he was saying seemed to sink in and her expression softened. "I'm not sure I understand."

"I'm sure you do."

She didn't deny his claim, just glanced toward her sleeping mother, then took on a resolved look.

"I was practically engaged in college," she told him. "His name was Tony and we were crazy about each other. We were going to graduate with our nursing degrees and sign on to be travel nurses and go around the world together."

She walked over to the foot of her mother's bed, straightened a wrinkle in the quilt that covered her.

"Everything was wonderful until Momma got so sick and quit working. She'd made a mess of her bills, taken out loans against the house, and was on the verge of losing everything. I moved home, took on extra hours waitressing at the restaurant where we went that first night, and somehow managed to keep going to school and keep my scholarship."

"I've said it before and I'll say it again—you are the strongest woman I know."

"I feel weak," she admitted. "I feel weak that I wanted you so much that I carried on with you at the hospital and pretended it meant nothing because I didn't want to stop. I feel weak that I didn't make you stay away, that I wasn't strong enough to stop this before it got started, before emotions got all tangled up." She paused, took a deep breath. "I feel weak that I'm not able to juggle all this so I can keep you in my life."

She stopped, closed her eyes. "I feel weak that I want you so much that I want to just forget everything else and be with you."

"Carly," he began, but she held up her hand.

"I'm not that person, Stone. I'm not somebody who can turn her back on someone she loves and I love my momma." Her face became pained. "The problem is, I love you, too."

Carly couldn't believe she'd said the words out loud. That she'd just told Stone that she was in love with him.

That he hadn't run out of the room. Or laughed in her face.

Instead, he stood next to her mother's hospital bed and just stared at her.

"I'm not sure what I'm supposed to say to that, Carly. Am I supposed to tell you that I'm sorry you love me?"

She swallowed the knot forming in her throat.

"Because I'm not," he continued. "Maybe I should be since it obviously stresses you, but I'm not," he repeated, his gaze searching hers as he walked to her, placed his hands on her shoulders and stared down into her eyes. "I want you to love me, Carly," he admitted. "Even when part of me doesn't want to complicate your life or add to your stress or to tie your future down, I want you to love me."

She trembled within his hold, then whatever walls were still in place crumbled and, tears running down her cheeks, she leaned against him. "I'm sorry, Stone," she mumbled against his chest. "I'm sorry I didn't tell you everything from the beginning, that I let things happen between us when we can't be together. Not now or ever because I can't bear the thought of asking you to wait."

Stone hugged Carly, breathed in her sweet scent, wanted to freeze time to this moment when she was safe in his arms.

Unfortunately, he couldn't.

And maybe he didn't really want to, because there were still things between him and Carly that needed to be removed.

"I need to tell you about that baggage I once mentioned." He took a deep breath. "I got married while in graduate school."

Carly jerked out of his arms, gawked up at him, her expression one full of betrayal. "You're married?"

"Divorced," he corrected. "We didn't make it a full year."

She was confused, her expression softening. "What happened?"

"I didn't love her, but…she was pregnant and marriage was the right thing. I wanted to help her, to make things better for her and our baby. It's what I planned to do. What I tried to do."

Mind obviously blown, she choked out, "You have a child?"

He shook his head. "No. She miscarried."

Carly winced and Stone had to take a deep, steadying breath to be able to continue.

"I wanted to help her, Carly. I really did. I could see she was struggling with her pregnancy and the changes to her life. But she kept pushing me away because she knew I didn't love her. She says I willed her to have a miscarriage because I didn't want a wife and child."

Carly's eyes were wide, her jaw slack, her expression one of shock. "Oh."

"Yeah, oh. She was already battling depression and the miscarriage compounded everything." He sucked in another deep breath. "She refused everything I tried to do. I could see how bad things were for her, but she blamed me for her problems and wouldn't let me in."

"Like what I did, even though it was my fault for not nipping our attraction in the bud," Carly mused, pacing across the room as she tried to work through the things he was telling her. "I really am sorry, Stone."

What had happened with Carly was nothing like what had happened with Stephanie. It had taken him a while and overhearing her conversation with Rosalyn to realize that. But he had realized it.

"When Stephanie divorced me…" He shrugged. "I felt I'd failed her, that I hadn't been able to help her and was guilty. I married her because I wanted to make her life better and I just ended up making everything worse. Just as I wanted to make things better for you, but ended up making things worse. I didn't plan to ever marry again, Carly, but you need me."

"Don't," she stopped him, shaking her head emphatically back and forth from where she stood across the room. "Don't offer to marry me to solve my problems. It's what you did with her, why your marriage fell apart, because it was for all the wrong reasons. Don't make the same mistake twice."

"That's not what I was going to do."

"Isn't it?" she challenged. "You're a good man. A man who has a big heart and wants to help those in need. It's what makes you such a great surgeon. But I don't need you playing the role of superhero in my life. I really can manage okay on my own."

"I know you can, Carly." She could do anything she set her mind to. She truly was the strongest woman he'd ever met. "But haven't you heard a thing I've said? I want it all. The good, the bad, I'll take it all if it means having you."

Carly's lower lip disappeared between her teeth at the same time as fresh tears streamed down her face. "I can't let you do that."

"Can't let me be with the person I want to be with?"

She began pacing again, still shaking her head. "You have no idea what you're offering to take on, the cost, the emotional and physical burden."

"I'm a doctor, Carly. I have some idea." He crossed to where she stood, took her hand into his, and dropped to one knee. "Marry me, Carly. I've been lost without you. Say yes, quit the insurance job." He shrugged. "Quit both jobs and stay with your mother, and let me take care of both of you."

She didn't answer him, just cupped his face with her free hand and asked, "Why would you want to do that?"

"Why?" He laughed self-derisively. "Because I love you."

* * *

Carly's body lifted with joy at Stone's words. He loved her. How could that even be?

Yet even as excitement filled her she quelled it and closed her eyes.

"Saying yes would be taking advantage of how wonderful you are. How can I do that and not feel guilty?"

"Taking care of you would make me happier than you can imagine."

"You won't leave me?" she asked, not quite able to believe what was happening.

"Never."

She stared at him for long moments, saw the truth in his eyes. There were so many unknowns in life, so many things that could change in the blink of an eye. Anything worth having came with risks.

Love came with risks.

Looking into Stone's eyes, holding tightly onto his hand, trusting in him, didn't feel risky.

It felt right.

"I love you, Stone."

"That's why I'm here. Once I set my wounded pride aside, it didn't take much for me to realize you had strong feelings for me. Otherwise, you wouldn't have risked everything to be with me."

"I think I loved you from the moment we met."

"You going to answer my question?"

She smiled, caressed his face, and nodded. "Yes."

"A-about t-time."

Both Carly and Stone spun toward the bed.

"Momma! I didn't know you were awake."

"G-glad I w-woke up."

"Miss Evans, I'd like your permission to marry Carly."

"B-bit l-late t-to b-be asking th-that," her mother slurred. "B-but, y-yes."

Carly hugged her mother, so grateful to see the recognition in her eyes that she'd not seen in days. She wasn't sure how long it would last, but she'd enjoy every precious second.

Just as she'd enjoy every precious second with the man she'd been blessed to love and be loved by.

EPILOGUE

CARLY AND STONE married a month later in Carly's back-yard. The weather was perfect, as was the day.

Carly's mother knew who she was, knew what was happening, that Carly was marrying her best friend.

Stone had arranged repairs to the outside of the house that had included a new roof and fresh paint. He'd had the landscaping redone with lots of vivid flowers that brightened its appearance, and had even surprised her with two white rocking chairs to put on the front porch with the ferns he'd hung.

Gone was the neglect and in its place was happiness and a new beginning. One where they would live in Carly's home to care for her mother, after which time they'd decide where they wanted to live, what they wanted to do.

Carly had kept her job at the hospital, but had quit the insurance claims job so she had time to spend with her mother, and with Stone.

Stone's family, Rosalyn, Joyce, and several of Stone's friends were in attendance at the small ceremony in Carly's backyard and celebrated there with them after the vow exchange.

Carly had never been hugged so much as she had that day by Stone's family, by his parents, his sisters, nephews and nieces, by his friends.

When he finally rescued her from them and pulled her into his arms, he grinned down at her.

"Hello, Mrs. Parker. Anyone told you how beautiful you are today?"

Heart full of love, Carly nodded. "Almost everyone here."

He smiled. "You are beautiful, Carly."

He made her feel beautiful. That day and every day after.

* * * * *

MILLS & BOON

Coming soon

BOUND TO THE
SICILIAN'S BED
Sharon Kendrick

Rocco was going to kiss her and after everything she'd just said, Nicole knew she needed to stop him. But suddenly she found herself governed by a much deeper need than preserving her sanity, or her pride. A need and a hunger which swept over her with the speed of a bush fire. As Rocco's shadowed face lowered towards her she found past and present fusing, so that for a disconcerting moment she forgot everything except the urgent hunger in her body. Because hadn't her Sicilian husband always been able to do this—to captivate her with the lightest touch and to tantalise her with that smouldering look of promise? And hadn't there been many nights since they'd separated when she'd woken up, still half fuddled with sleep, and found herself yearning for the taste of his lips on hers just one more time? And now she had it.

One more time.

She opened her mouth—though afterwards she would try to convince herself she'd been intending to resist him—but Rocco used the opportunity to fasten his mouth over hers in the most perfects of fits. And Nicole felt instantly helpless—caught up in the powerful snare of a sexual mastery which wiped out everything else. She gave a gasp of pleasure because it had been so long since she had done this.

Since they'd been apart Nicole had felt like a living statue—as if she were made from marble—as if the flesh and blood part of her were some kind of half-forgotten dream. Slowly but surely she had withdrawn from the sensual side of her nature, until she'd convinced herself she was dead and unfeeling inside. But here came Rocco to wake her dormant sexuality with nothing more than a single kiss. It was like some stupid fairy story. It was scary and powerful. She didn't *want* to want him, and yet . . .

She wanted him.

Her lips opened wider as his tongue slid inside her mouth—eagerly granting him that intimacy as if preparing the way for another. She began to shiver as his hands started to explore her—rediscovering her body with an impatient hunger, as if it were the first time he'd ever touched her.

'Nicole,' he said unevenly and she'd never heard him say her name like that before.

Her arms were locked behind his neck as again he circled his hips in unmistakable invitation and, somewhere in the back of her mind, Nicole could hear the small voice of reason imploring her to take control of the situation. It was urging her to pull back from him and call a halt to what they were doing. But once again she ignored it. Against the powerful tide of passion, that little voice was drowned out and she allowed pleasure to shimmer over her skin.

Continue reading
BOUND TO THE SICILIAN'S BED
Sharon Kendrick

Available next month
www.millsandboon.co.uk

LET'S TALK
Romance

For exclusive extracts, competitions
and special offers, find us online:

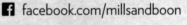

facebook.com/millsandboon

@millsandboonuk

@millsandboon

Or get in touch on 0844 844 1351*

For all the latest titles coming soon, visit
millsandboon.co.uk/nextmonth

Want even more
ROMANCE?

Join our bookclub today!

'Mills & Boon books, the perfect way to escape for an hour or so.'

Miss W. Dyer

'Excellent service, promptly delivered and very good subscription choices.'

Miss A. Pearson

'You get fantastic special offer and the chance to get books before they hit the shops'

Mrs V Hall

Visit millsandbook.co.uk/Bookclub
and save on brand new books.

MILLS & BOON